'I'm going to ... and this time ...

Casey met Dylan's ~~steady gaze.~~ 'No,' she said, but all around her came the lapping silence of the northern woods, and the knowledge that she *couldn't* get away from him—not for weeks and weeks. 'Making love wasn't on the agenda, MacCabe.'

'Yeah, well, that's the thing about travel,' he said in frustration. 'It's full of surprises.'

'Keep your surprises to yourself. This is business.'

· 'Casey, we could light up most of Bridgewater with the electricity between us.' He lowered his voice. 'You feel it, too.'

She bristled. 'I didn't come out here looking for a lover.'

'Neither did I, but now it's happened.' He paused, and she could hear him breathing. Waiting. 'Look at me, Casey.'

Knowing it was a mistake, she twisted abruptly and looked straight into those intense blue eyes. A shiver passed through her that had nothing to do with cold or fear, and everything to do with passion—a passion she didn't want to feel. Yet standing before him, she knew it was inevitable...

Dear Reader,

Although I have written several historical romances, *Loving Wild* is my very first venture into the exciting world of Temptation®.

I love writing romance—in fact, I just love writing. Despite what my friends suspect, I didn't become a writer, and thus sidetrack a promising career as a chemist, so that I would never have to wear tights. My motives were much more subversive. You see, in the 'real' world, I'm afraid of flying, I hate driving at night and I willingly watch from the safety of a bench while my children hurl through the air on rollercoasters. But in fiction I boldly fly F-14s, float gloriously in hot air balloons, brashly face down bad guys and—as in *Loving Wild*—I canoe uncharted rapids with a tall, handsome, lusty man who has more than survival on his mind.

On top of it all, I get to take you, the reader, on the journey with me. Please—let me know if you like the ride. You can drop me a line at Harlequin Books, 225 Duncan Mill Road, Don Mills, Ontario, Canada, M3B 3K9.

Wishing you many exciting journeys,

Lisa Ann Verge

LOVING WILD

by

Lisa Ann Verge

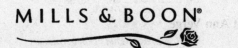

MILLS & BOON®

MILLS & BOON and MILLS & BOON with the Rose Device are registered trademarks of the publisher. TEMPTATION is a registered trademark of Harlequin Enterprises Limited, used under licence.

First published in Great Britain 1998 by Harlequin Mills & Boon Limited, Eton House, 18-24 Paradise Road, Richmond, Surrey TW9 1SR

© Lisa Ann Verge 1998

ISBN 0 263 81410 6

21-9810

Printed and bound in Great Britain by Caledonian International Book Manufacturing Ltd, Glasgow

1

"C'MON, BESSIE, HOLD ON for me." Casey Michaels patted the dashboard of her three-year-old minivan as it lurched over a rut in the dirt road. "That cabin can't be far now. I'll be sure to give this nature boy a good talking-to about the virtues of a telephone...if I ever lay eyes on him."

Casey pressed the brake as she approached a fork in the path. The rays of the sun blazed in dappled confusion across the windshield. She opened a crinkled map against the steering wheel and trailed her fingernail over the razor-thin line she'd been following for the past half hour, comparing the map to the maze of dirt roads she'd just navigated.

She chewed on her lower lip and tried to ignore the niggle of panic in her belly. Her gaze flickered to the dashboard clock. She had been driving for nine hours. Her lower back throbbed from sitting in the lumpy seat. Her leg ached from pressing on the gas. But she needed this assignment too badly to turn back now simply because she was lost in the wilds of the Adirondack Mountains with a dying vehicle.

"Isn't it just my luck, to be assigned to find Davy Crockett," she muttered, massaging the cramp in her right thigh. This was the age of portable fax machines, cellular phones, e-mail and the World Wide Web. Yet this guy had buried himself so deep in the woods that she doubted he could even see smoke signals.

Which made it all the more likely, she reminded herself, that he would grant her an exclusive on his story.

She concentrated on the map. Yes, she remembered that turnoff. And that riding trail that crossed the road. She shoved the map aside. Okay. She flexed her fingers around the steering wheel. There was no reason to be even a tiny bit worried. So Bessie was shaking like an old washing machine. Bessie had clocked—Casey checked the odometer—over eighty thousand miles. The trusty minivan could certainly do a few miles more.

Easing the van down the left fork, she cracked her elbow on the side window when Bessie lurched through a rut. As she grimaced with pain, she reminded herself that she'd been in worse positions than this. Like the time Bessie overheated in the Mojave Desert. Then, of course, Casey had had a healthy bank account, and hadn't cringed at the cost of a tow truck and car repairs. Lately, her bank balance came in the low four digits, and it was sinking fast.

She might have missed the squat little building a half mile down the road if it hadn't been for the flash of sun off the Jeep parked in front of it. She lurched Bessie to an unsteady stop and peered through the trees. Yes...that was it. It *had* to be it. The cabin stood far back from the road, sheltered under a canopy of spruce, its weathered logs the same rusty color as the trunks of the trees surrounding it.

It looked like the kind of place where this guy would live, she thought, as she turned into the graveled driveway and shut off the van with a symphony of coughs and sputters. She dragged her battered leather briefcase onto her lap and fingered through her papers until she found her yellow pad with the notes from yesterday's conversation with her editor. This was the kind of guy, she mused, perusing her notes, who would spend a year making a birchbark canoe, and a summer paddling blindly into the wilderness.

Reaching behind her, Casey tugged her boxy linen jacket out from under a pile of books, slipped her arms into its cool lining, and stepped out of the van. She heard the distinct sound of someone chopping wood behind the cabin. Davy Crockett, no doubt. Stocking up on heating fuel for the long winter. She hoped he believed in jumper cables, or she would never get Bessie out of his front yard.

Shoving her sunglasses up the bridge of her nose, she picked her way around the cabin and told herself that he could be the most unpleasant tobacco-spitting, beer-drinking, unshaven, plaid-shirt-wearing lout but she would stay—gleefully—if it meant he would grant her an interview.

As she reached the clearing behind the cabin, she stopped short. The remains of a very thick tree lay scattered across the ground. In the midst of the carnage stood a man with a pair of the widest shoulders she'd ever seen. As she watched, the six-foot wonder hefted a flashing ax and hurled it toward a defenseless little log.

She thought it prudent to wait until the axe had sliced into the wood before speaking.

"Excuse me...Mr. MacCabe?"

The man straightened and glanced over his shoulder. He had light, piercing eyes. A Viking's eyes. To go with the shimmer of blond the sun had bleached in his hair. The piercing gaze raked over her with a thoroughness that left her feeling rumpled and bare.

"Yeah," he said, shoving a log out of the way with his foot. "I'm MacCabe. You lost?"

"No...no. It seems I've just found who I'm looking for." She slung her bag over her shoulder and picked her way across the clearing, trying not to wince as she eased weight on her cramped leg. "I hope I'm not disturbing you. I didn't intend to drop by unexpectedly. But you don't have a phone...."

"I like surprises better."

She stood closer now. She met his eyes. A jarringly bright blue. In a face well-tanned and leathery.

Under the heat of that gaze, Casey tightened her grip on the strap of her bag. She wrote for a number of sports and adventure magazines, so she knew the "look": MacCabe was sun-bronzed with health, lean and muscular from outdoor sports, and not shy about wearing biker's shorts and tank tops to their best advantage. In the three years she'd freelanced, she'd long since grown used to interviewing sweaty, half-dressed, well-built males.

But most of the men she interviewed were verging on their twenty-fifth birthdays. And most of those took one look at her thirty-two-year-old face and, with the cruelty of youth, called her "ma'am."

She would be hearing no "ma'am" from Dylan Mac-Cabe. Despite his muscular good looks, the man standing before her with a curious gleam in his eye was no young adventurer. The beginnings of crow's feet fanned out from his eyes. His hair, a tousled brown burnished gold by the sun and obviously having outgrown its last cut, showed at the temples a few strands of silver.

And Dylan MacCabe was more...hardened. Almost grizzled, in a comfortably attractive, bearish sort of way. Probably in his late thirties, if she could gauge age at all.

Then she realized she was staring. Rudely. And he was watching her stare with a twitch of his lips. She managed an apologetic smile, hoped she wasn't blushing, and thrust out her hand. "The name's Casey Michaels."

He engulfed her hand in his own—a hand that was warm and big and rough with bits of wood. It held hers in a dangerously easy and comfortable fit. She struggled with the unexpected feeling of being tugged along by it, though he made no move at all.

Her heart made a sudden leap in her chest—a strange, fearful little jump. She realized with piercing clarity that she was alone with this giant of a man in a place where only the squirrels would hear her scream. Then, just as quickly, she chided herself for having read too many horror novels.

"Hello, Casey Michaels." He drew out the word *hello*. "Whatever you're selling, it's sure that you're the best thing that has happened to me all day."

"Oh?" She quickly snatched her hand away, wondering why she had, a moment after she did it. "You're not having trouble with the trip, I hope?"

He raised his brows. "You know about the trip?"

"It's the reason why I'm here. I'm a freelance writer, Mr. MacCabe."

She rifled in her bag, searching for a business card. Her hair slid down across her face and she took the moment to gather her wits. He didn't fit the usual description of her subjects. Of course, she was accustomed to dealing with good-looking guys. She'd interviewed some of the most appealing bachelors in the country, much to the envy of her unmarried sisters. Whenever she dropped the name of the latest sports hunk, she had always smiled tolerantly at their melodramatic swoons and wide-eyed giddiness. They claimed she had ice in her veins. But she'd long ago come to terms with the fact that she just wasn't capable of feeling that way about a man—not anymore.

A familiar tightness gripped her chest. She took a deep breath and forced it loose. This was not the time to be thinking of the past. She had Bessie to think of, and her own uncertain future.

"Here it is." Casey tugged a black business card out of her bag. "I've been sent here by *American Backroads*."

"I know the magazine." He tugged the card from her hand. She watched the way his hair tumbled over his brow as he eyed the rainbow-foil print. "It always has some guy in neon spandex on the front cover."

"That's it. It's a monthly. They cover everything from hang gliding to bungee jumping to, most recently, a re-creation of the trip over the Oregon Trail." Was she babbling? She felt strangely as if she were babbling, even though this was her usual pitch. "My editor got your name from the local geographical alliance. She loves what you're doing. She thinks it would be the kind of journey the subscribers would like to read about."

"And you've been assigned to write it up."

"A full feature article, for the October edition." She tapped her pen on her yellow pad of paper. "Providing no one else has beaten me to you, of course. We'll insist on an exclusive."

She clicked the nib of her pen. Her throat tightened as she waited for him to pick up on the opening. Waiting to see if she would have enough cash to repair Bessie's C. V. joints before they busted. Waiting to see if she would be able to fi-nance her wanderlust lifestyle another week longer, an-other day longer, another hour longer. Anything to stave off the reality of her financial situation: If she didn't get a steady stream of well-paying assignments soon, she'd be forced to get a nine-to-five job, to settle somewhere, estab-lish roots again.

Maybe even go home.

But Dylan MacCabe remained thoughtfully silent, finger-ing the edges of the business card. He eyed the gold chain at her neck and the lines of her linen suit. Then his gaze fol-lowed her hosed legs all the way down to her sensible tan leather pumps.

She stood there in the hot August sun while a prickly

heat that had nothing to do with the weather crept up her neck. She watched his face from behind the guard of her sunglasses, wondering if she had runs in her pearly stockings. And feeling, all of a sudden, very small, very vulnerable...very feminine.

Feminine. Intensely aware of her bare throat, the tickle of her hair upon the nape of her neck, the press of her breasts against the silken fibers of her blouse.

He swiped the hem of his tank top in a fist, then slid the business card between his black shorts and glistening skin. "You're not local, are you, Casey?"

"Local? Oh, no." She fixed her gaze on the sweat gleaming in the hollow of his throat. It seemed a safe enough place to look, since her eyes were hidden behind her sunglasses; safer than at the edge of the business card peeping above his waistband. "I work stories all over," she explained. "I just finished a piece on a cross-country hike from Hudson Bay to the St. Lawrence River."

There, she thought. Professional credentials confirmed. Maybe that was why he was giving her such a once-over. She couldn't imagine why else. It was true that she did cover what was usually considered a man's beat. Casey remembered how one of the ladies at her hometown paper used to complain that the editors always farmed her off to the women's club monthly meeting and the board of education budget stories—and never let her in on the hot local scoops. But Casey freelanced. She chose her own stories, on her own whims. Personally, she had never experienced any sort of discrimination.

She wasn't even sure she was experiencing it now. She wasn't quite sure what she was experiencing.

"You've come all the way down from Canada," he asked, wiping his face with a fistful of tank top, "just to cover me?"

"Don't be flattered, Mr. MacCabe," she said. "I've traveled farther to catch a story."

"Still, that's a long way to come, just to write about a little canoe trip."

"I wouldn't call it that." Casey flipped up her yellow pad again, twisting it to read her scribble though she knew darned well what it said. "A 'little' canoe trip through the Adirondack wilderness, tracing old trading routes?"

"I'm surprised you found me at all." He dropped the hem of his tank top and scraped his hand over the faded sports logo. "We've been here for weeks, without a phone."

"You weren't so hard to find," she lied, shrugging. "I called the contact number the alliance gave my editor. Your partner's wife faxed me directions to this cabin."

"Directions?" He flashed her a hundred-watt grin. "What, turn at the split oak and veer left at the creek?"

"Well...they weren't too good," she admitted. "But the park ranger gave me a map." She shrugged and clicked the pen again. "I often find myself bumbling down dirt roads. It's the nature of the job."

He eyed her in that strange speculative way again.

"Reporters can be very resourceful, Mr. MacCabe."

"I see that." He disarmed her with another bright grin. "And call me Dylan. Otherwise I'll start treating you like one of my high-school students."

She managed a tight smile to match his much warmer one. She was beginning to feel like a high-school student. Giddy and strangely jumpy, and all because this six-foot Viking had given her a once-over as invigorating as a Swedish massage.

"Listen, we're going to be on this trip for three weeks," he said, dipping down to heft a log under his arm. "Are you going to hang around until it's done?"

She blinked at him. "Does that mean you're giving me—the magazine—an exclusive?"

He glanced around the clearing, then looked at her with a comic tilt of his head. "Well, there's not a heck of a lot of competition waiting here, for the chance to grant me my fifteen minutes of fame."

The pressure in her chest eased, and she felt the swift unraveling of muscles coiled too long and too tight. She sucked in a quick, deep breath and felt it rush all the way down to her toes. She hadn't realized she'd been holding her breath.

She started making swift calculations. A feature article could run up to three thousand words. That could finance a couple of weeks' frugal travel, minus Bessie's mechanic's bills, if she spent a few nights in her van. She might also be able to write a shorter piece about the trip, with a different angle, for a smaller magazine.

Then she realized she was grinning idiotically at the man who had paused, mid-crouch in his wood gathering, at the sound of her gasp of relief. She thought back on their conversation until she remembered what he had asked her, before he'd unwittingly granted her several more weeks of freedom. Was she going to stay?

"Three weeks," she said, slapping her yellow pad on the back of her hand, just to do something with the sudden surge of nervous energy. "I don't know. It depends on the story. And you." She paused in her rhythmic slapping as a thought came to her. "But I have no intention of being an imposition, Mr. MacCabe, if that's what you're worried about—"

"Dylan." He shoved another log into the stack tucked under his arm. "And believe me, any lady who looks like you is no imposition."

Her smile froze on her face even as the rest of her body hummed like a hive of bees.

"So," he continued, as if his words hadn't turned her into a human tuning fork, "you're telling me you have no plans for the next three weeks?"

"My schedule is...fluid," she said, her ears still buzzing. "I adjust it however I need to."

Of course, she had no intention of staying the full three weeks. She couldn't afford the hotel bills, and she would only suffer sleeping in her van for a few days at a time. She needed to get this story done right, and done soon, and then move on.

Besides, she never spent more time than she needed in any one place. It always took about four or five days of contact before people stopped answering her questions and started asking some of their own. About *her*—her life, her past, her dreams. A sure indicator that it was time for her to hit the road in search of the next story. Life was more simple—and less painful—when it didn't involve intimate relationships.

Especially with broad-shouldered, warm-eyed men like this one, who kept sizing her up...for something.

"Well," she said, clicking her pen and tapping it against the yellow pad, "do you want to start by telling me about some of the problems you've been having?"

"It's nothing. Yet." He straightened and hefted the wood toward a wrought-iron brace against the cabin wall. "Just the usual annoyances that plague big projects right before they start."

"I like details. I need details. They're what bring the story to life." She looked around the yard, at the splatter of cut wood, then pointedly at the screened back door of the cabin. "If you can spare a few minutes from this, maybe we could settle down somewhere and talk."

"Let me finish piling this up first."

He patted the ends of the logs to line them up evenly, then returned without another word to gather more. She glanced at the wood, then at the empty brace. Her reporter's instincts told her there was something fishy here—Dylan was dodging telling her something. But it was quite obvious there was no rushing the man.

She decided to let it go, for now. She tucked the yellow pad back into her bag. Truth be told, she needed a little time to gather her wits. Maybe it was the pressure she'd put on herself, driving so far and so long in the hopes of snagging this story, but even though she'd gotten a guarantee on an exclusive, she still felt strangely unsettled.

She wandered around the clearing, concentrating on the soft crinkle of pine needles under her shoes, the warmth of the sun filtering through the trees, the sound of the logs clattering into the brace. These northern summer woods reminded her of the retreat she had stayed at, three years ago. She'd spent hours wandering those well-tended grounds, losing herself among the trees, trying to put herself and her life back together again.

"This is pretty country," she said, shoving her hands into the pockets of her jacket. "Is the cabin yours?"

"It belongs to my family," he said, straightening to eye the surrounding woods. "We spent every summer here."

"We?"

"My parents, two brothers and a sister." His grin flashed. "Imagine, two adults and four kids in a two-room cabin. Funny, it never seemed crowded."

Her gaze drifted toward the cabin as she imagined the blur of children playing hide-and-seek, catching toads, swinging on low limbs, running wild. If she had ever had children, she would have wanted to raise them in a place like this.

She took a swift, deep breath and cast about for some other focus. She set her sights on a strange-looking canoe, up on struts by the side of the house.

As she neared the canoe, she smelled turpentine and something else she couldn't place.

"Careful," he said, as she reached out to touch it. "That black stuff is pine tar and it's hellish to get off your hands."

"This must be the canoe you made."

"Yeah, that's it."

She patted the stiff side, avoiding the sticky resin. "Is it really made out of tree bark?"

"Yellow birch bark." He straightened with a bunch of wood tucked under his arm. "It's made as the Native Americans used to make it. What do you know about this trip?"

"Next to nothing," she admitted. She dug a thumb under the strap of her briefcase. "This particular editor likes to send me off blind, just to see what I can come up with."

"Sounds like a hell of a career." Dylan tucked another log into the pile under his arm. "Bungee jumping, following the Oregon Trail, hang gliding—"

"I don't actually *do* any of those things," she assured him with a laugh. "I just write about them. There was one guy who tried to get me to bungee jump, but there was no way on earth I was going to leap off a bridge with a rope tied around my feet."

"That's just good common sense." He paused in his wood gathering. "So you've never participated in anything you've covered?"

"No, I've done a few things. I did take part in a white-water trip on the Snake River, with a bunch of crazy executives trying to learn 'teamwork.'"

"You rafted the Snake River?"

"Well...not really. I paddled a ways down the river with

them, just to get a feel for it. But I opted out of running the real white water." She straightened her shoulders, determined to shift this interview to him, for a change. "Did you make this canoe all by yourself, Mr. MacCabe?"

"Yeah—no. I had a lot of help." He shoved some more wood into the last gap of the wrought-iron brace. "Some of the kids in my American history class helped. Why didn't you join those executives for the whole trip, Casey?"

She blinked at him. He had made his way across the yard and now was standing in front of her, his hands on his hips, his abdomen caving in with every exhaled breath. She felt a sudden exquisite consciousness of his state of undress—of the expanse of chest, covered by nothing more than a damp tank top that molded to his upper body, the biker's shorts hugging his thighs. Sweat had darkened the curls of his hair and plastered them to his neck.

"I just cover the stories, Mr. MacCabe," she said, her throat suddenly dry. "I don't live them myself."

That was the only answer she would give him. He didn't need to know the truth. He didn't need to know that this was as close to risk as she wanted to get—for now.

"You look as if you could handle any physical demands." His gaze swept over her again. "Do you work out?"

"Excuse me?"

"You know." He waved a hand in the air. "Weights. Aerobics. Step classes."

"I run," she said, as if it were any of his business. She had pounded the pavement from San Francisco to the boardwalks of Atlantic City, from the river walks of the Mississippi to the Mojave Desert. It was the one thing she hadn't yet given up from her old life. "I try to make a habit of jogging three times a week. Now, if you've quizzed me enough on my qualifications, Mr. MacCabe, I'd really like to ask *you* a few questions."

He laughed. It was a kind sound, and a dangerous sound. A deep, sexy rumble from the chest.

"Socratic method," he explained. "It's the way I teach my students. It's a habit that's hard to break."

She still couldn't believe he was a high-school teacher. He looked more like he belonged in a wet suit on the beaches of southern California. Or shark fishing off the Great Barrier reefs of Australia.

"This canoe," she said, turning toward it so she wouldn't have to look at him and the whorls of dark hair converging upon the waistband of his shorts, "you'll be taking it all the way through the wilderness?"

"Casey," he said, as if she hadn't spoken a word, "I have a confession to make."

She glanced back at him, startled, and found herself riveted by that bright blue stare again. Confession? He didn't look in the least bit guilty. He looked sweaty and hard-bodied. Intense. A vein throbbed on the inside of his arm. His chest rose and fell with deep, steady regularity.

"Danny—Daniel Anderson, my partner in this ill-fated voyage of mine—is in the hospital right now."

"What?"

"He's all right." He watched her face intently. "But he broke his arm water-skiing yesterday."

"Oh." She dug her hand into her bag, searching blindly for her yellow pad. Her instincts had never been wrong. Now, it seemed, she was finally getting somewhere with this story—and the sooner the better. "So...is this one of those setbacks you didn't want to talk about?"

"Yeah." He grinned and shrugged in a way that would look boyish in a younger man. "But it's not a setback anymore."

"Your partner is in the hospital. I'd call that a setback. I trust you have someone else to take his place?"

"I hope so."

She blinked at him, pausing in her search for her pad of paper. What did he mean, he hoped so? He'd promised her an exclusive on this trip—he'd better have a substitute, or all her hopes of getting Bessie new C. V. joints went right out the window, along with a lot of other half-baked plans.

"Call me crazy, Casey, but watching you walk up to me a few minutes ago was like seeing the answer to my prayers."

The yellow pad slipped out of her hand and sank into the recesses of her leather bag.

"I've been standing here, cracking wood, trying to think of a way out of this situation." He shook his head. "Eight months of planning, and good old Danny-boy has to show off to his eldest son by playing acrobat on the ski jump three days before the launch."

Casey sank her heel into the soft mulch of the ground as Dylan took a step toward her.

"And then," he continued, "with no warning, I turn around to find this strong, confident woman standing there, a woman who has run white water before, and who has nothing planned for the next three weeks."

"I didn't say—"

"I'm offering you a great challenge. I'm giving you the chance to live one of your own stories." He leaned into her. "Casey Michaels...how would you like to join me on the adventure of a lifetime?"

2

CASEY HAD ONCE BEEN sent on assignment to California, to cover a surfboarding competition off the beaches of La Jolla. She'd been enticed into paddling out into the water for what the surfer boys called an "easy ride." As she'd attempted to stand on the board, a wave had swept it out beneath her, plunged her into the water, scraped her across the bottom, then spat her out onto the shore. For minutes uncounted she had lain flat on her back, staring up at the blue sky, wondering what the devil had hit her.

She knew what had hit her this time. It was looming over her, grinning like a Cheshire cat, brawny arms akimbo, focusing all that blue-eyed intensity upon her. She just didn't know why she was shaking even though she knew she was standing flat-footed on the ground.

"Let me get this straight," she said, taking another step back into the crush of the pine needles. "You want me to be your partner."

"Yep."

"Just like that."

"You're perfect," he insisted, as his gaze swept her from top to toe. "Lighter than I expected for a sternsman, but I can balance out the packs to compensate—"

"If I refuse to be your partner," she interrupted, wishing he would stop breathing down on her, "does that mean the trip is canceled?"

"Well..."

"It's over, isn't it?"

"Unless someone else with nothing to do for the next three weeks comes walking around my cabin—"

"Then it seems," she said, fingering her sunglasses back up the bridge of her nose, "that your trip is off, Mr. Mac-Cabe. A pleasure to speak to you. Good day."

She twisted on one sensible heel and headed away from him. She fixed her gaze on the corner post of the cabin. She fixed her mind on the sanctuary of her van just beyond.

Heavy footsteps crackled in the litter behind her.

"No way, MacCabe." She swept out an arm before he came too close. Her jacket fluttered with the wind of her pace. "I came here to write about the trip, not live it. Our business is done."

"You haven't even heard what I have to say."

"I've heard all I needed to hear."

"Will you stop running?"

"I'm not running."

She felt like running. She felt like lurching into a sprint as she rounded the cabin and caught sight of her van. If she'd been wearing better shoes, she just might have.

Because Dylan MacCabe had just spent the past half-hour giving her hope—and the past few minutes destroying it.

Nine hours of driving, no assignment, the minivan worse for the trip, and she was left wondering how she would eke out a living with the last of the settlement money before she would have to make some hard, hard decisions about her life.

She reached out and curled her fingers under the hot metal of the door handle. She pulled on the latch.

"Hold it, Casey."

The door clicked open. Dylan's shadow fell over her. He slammed his hands on the door, jamming it shut.

He had work-worn hands. Rough hands. Big hands. Lying flat on the window of her car, on either side of her head. She stood there with her breath coming fast between her lips, staring into the window, into the comfortable clutter of her van, and seeing little else but the reflection of the Viking in the glass as he leaned into her, close enough for her to feel his breath on her hair.

"You really are a runner, aren't you?"

The words shot through her like a bullet. She supposed, by the way he said them—with a sort of rueful admiration—that he meant them as a compliment: that she had a strong set of legs and could run like the wind when she had to. But Casey's therapist had said the very same words to her, a couple of weeks ago, and Jillian had meant much, much more than that.

Well, she wasn't a runner anymore, Casey said to herself, just as she had told Jillian. She was a writer who traveled a lot—with reason.

So she twisted around to face Dylan—to confront, and thus take control of the situation—and realized immediately what a colossal mistake she'd made. Her shoulder brushed his chest as she turned. His face and his body were separated from hers by mere inches of air space.

And the air was thinning dangerously.

That strange sensation seized her again. The sensation of being tugged along, of being guided, urged, pushed... closer to him.

He didn't move. The world slowed around them. Casey noticed odd things. His bristled jaw. Golden bristles, speckled here and there with brown, short and cropped, as if he'd gone no more than a day without shaving. A streak of dirt slashed across his brow, as if he'd swiped it there with the back of his forearm. A ring of silver gray encircled the pupils of his blue eyes. The ring widened as his pupils constricted and his gaze fell to her lips.

"Just listen to me," he said softly, his gaze rising to her eyes again. "Five minutes, Casey. That's all I ask."

She licked her lips. His gaze followed the movement. She had no intention of joining this man on any trip, anywhere, anytime, anyhow. But she nodded, just to do something, just to make him say something so he wouldn't keep staring at her like that. She nodded, in the hopes that he would move away so she could breathe again.

He pushed himself away from her, took a step back into the sunlight. He raked a hand through his hair, then dropped it to his hip. She filled her lungs with air.

"I just finished chopping enough wood to last until the next millennium," he began, "trying to work this all out." He stepped back farther, until he bumped into the side of his own Jeep. Leaning against it, he crossed his legs at the ankle and scratched his head, wincing as he talked. "I was just about ready to throw in the towel."

Casey flattened her hands against the hot door of the van, letting the heat burn her palms.

"Since yesterday," he continued, "I've been trying to find someone to take Danny's place. I spent the night sitting at a pay phone in a diner just outside town, feeding it dimes while I called every high-school boy in my history classes, every football player I've coached for the past three years, every softball player on my spring team. Nothing came through. Every kid is either working, going to college in mid-August, or his parents forbid him to join me."

"You can't get student athletes to go," she said, huskily, "but you want me."

"Hey, I even tried my tag-football team, but they all have real jobs. And the other teachers in Bridgewater High...well, the ones I'd willingly invite are either on vacation, or have other plans. Casey, you are the only person I know on God's Green Earth who has three weeks in the summer with nothing else to do. And here you are, at my door."

"But there's where you're wrong," she said, hating the strange, fragile timbre of her voice. "I told you I have no other assignment, but I do have plans. I have a sister in Connecticut. I haven't seen her or her family in almost two years. She's expecting me to visit."

"Push it off until after the trip."

"School starts in September. I want to see my nieces."

"We'll be done a week before Labor Day."

"You're rather free about rearranging my social schedule," she retorted, holding on to the spurt of anger. "But I'll have another assignment in September."

"That sounds vague."

"Listen, Mr. MacCabe—"

"Dylan. This could be worth your while, Casey. You could get three or four articles out of this trip."

"That's spreading the leftovers rather thin."

"An article for *American Backroads*. Another for *Canoeing and Kayaking*, and an easy third for one of the educators' trade magazines."

The knowledge gave her pause. Three articles out of three weeks. That added up to a lot of car-repair bills.

"I've been working on this for eight months," he continued, leaning toward her. "Filling out the forms for grants. Gathering the materials to build the canoe. Doing research on the old trading routes in this part of the country. Practicing the paddle strokes in the Bridgewater river in the cold of March—"

"Mr. Mac— Dylan," she said, holding out the flattened palms of her hands, as if she could push him farther away.

"Listen, I sympathize, but Lewis and Clark had to deal with setbacks, as well."

"Lewis and Clark didn't have to be back at a teaching desk by September seventh."

"Do it yourself, then. What's stopping you?"

"The canoe's too big for one paddler. It would take twice as long to make the trip, and there's too much gear for one man to carry across portages easily. Every portage would take twice as long."

She patted her own padded shoulders. "Oh, yeah," she said, "these shoulders look like they can handle a lot of weight."

"It's not brute strength I need, it's another warm body— another paddle holder. I can carry the bulk of the weight, but there's still more. Bulk, not weight."

This was absurd. She couldn't believe he was even asking her. She couldn't believe he would even consider it. She couldn't believe she had to talk him out of it. She couldn't believe she was still standing here and not halfway to the highway.

"Dylan," she said, mustering as much calm as she could, "how long have you been training?"

"For this? The better part of a year—"

"Great. That's all I need to hear."

"Not physically. It doesn't take a hell of a lot of skill to use a paddle. I've been *preparing* to do it for a year. Research. Paperwork—"

"You'll be sleeping out in the wilderness, won't you?"

"Yeah."

"I don't like camping. I don't like mosquitos."

"That's what netting and chemicals are for."

"I don't cook over open fires."

"That's what propane stoves are for—there are fire rules in the park."

"I don't bone fish."

"We'll bring in our own rations. We're not exactly roughing it, Casey. There are rules about hunting and fishing up there."

"You keep talking 'we' as if this is a foregone conclusion."

"It's fate." A grin lurked at the corners of his mouth. "It has to be. It's just too perfect."

She resisted the urge to snort. There wasn't any such thing as "fate." Fate implied some sort of orderly sequence of events; fate required that life made some kind of sense. She'd long ago learned that life made no sense at all, that everyone was just stumbling blindly in the dark.

She was stumbling now. She still reeled from Dylan's offer. And through the haze of swirling confusion she kept hearing Jillian's calm voice.

"Take the risk, Casey. That's what life is all about. Risks. What are you afraid of?"

"I will not."

She spoke the words more to the voice in her head than to the man before her, but he heard. He pushed away from the Jeep.

"You're not going to let this one get away from you, are you, Casey?"

"What are you talking about?"

"If you don't join me, there won't be a trip, there won't be a story."

And there won't be pay, she thought ruefully. *And poor ol' Bessie might sputter out on me.*

"What are you afraid of, Casey? The trip?" He lowered his voice to a rumble. "Or me?"

She met his gaze. Bright blue, blazing blue, intense blue. He'd asked the question rhetorically, but she took it at face value. As she always had when Jillian had asked it. What was she afraid of? For all her protestations, Casey didn't particularly hate camping. She and her family had done it several times during her teenage summers, and she'd enjoyed the experience. Though she would always like clean sheets, running water and soft mattresses better, she supposed she could handle camping.

There was the element of danger. He wouldn't be doing this if there wasn't some risk involved in the trip. But she didn't know what that risk was, couldn't even imagine it. They hadn't gotten that far in the interview.

What are you afraid of, Casey? The trip? Or me?

She hazarded him a glance. Dylan MacCabe was a handsome man. Any other thirty-two-year-old woman would give a few teeth to spend three weeks in the wild alone with him. Maybe that was why she was so full of skitters. She hadn't thought that way about a man for over three long years.

She didn't *want* to think that way about a man, ever again.

"I'm no trained athlete, Dylan," she said, her voice whisper-thin. "I'd be a fool to agree to a trip I know nothing about, except that it's sure to be dangerous."

"It's not that dangerous."

"Sure. It's for wimps, that's why you're going."

The grin took hold, widened. "I'm not saying it doesn't have its challenges," he conceded, "but the challenges are more in finding the right way through the maze of waterways, than in lions, tigers, or bears." He shuffled in the gravel. Closer to her. "At least come inside and let me show you what we're going to do."

"What *you* are going to do, you mean."

"You've come all the way out here. You would have asked me about the details of the trip anyway, right?"

She narrowed her eyes. He was right, of course. Her day

was lost, in any case. If nothing came of this, she would have to find her way out of this wilderness, find a hotel, and spend the night wondering where her next dollar was coming from. And if he *did* manage to find another partner—other than herself—she would need to know some background about the trip before she wrote the story.

"Please, Casey," he said softly. "Just come in and listen."

Then he gave her that hundred-watt smile, and she was lost.

CASEY BLINKED JUST inside the door to the cabin while her eyes became accustomed to the sudden dimness. The interior smelled of coffee and wood ash. It was far roomier than she'd expected, and far more modern. A bank of kitchen appliances lined one wall. A long counter jutted out to split the cabin in two: the back half for the kitchen/dining room, the other for the living room, with barstools along the outer side for casual dining. Worn braided oval rugs cushioned a rocking chair by a wicker magazine rack, and decorated a hearthstone. Over the shelf of cabinets, she glimpsed a cast-iron wood-burning stove near the raw stone fireplace.

So much for Davy Crockett.

She closed the door behind her and banged her knuckles on a plaque hanging on the doorknob that said Gone Fishing. She shrugged off her linen jacket and hung it on a peg by the door, next to a splintered old fishing creel. A collection of rods of varied lengths hung across a row of hooks above.

"Don't mind them," Dylan explained, as she eyed the mounted fish gaping at her from all around the room, their measurements and the date neatly etched in the bronzed plaques below. "My father's a real fishing enthusiast."

She arched a brow. "I never would have guessed."

"Now that he's retired, he spends most of the season

here. Took a lot of arm-twisting, but my mother convinced him to let me and Danny have it for the week, to prepare for the trip."

"That was generous of him." She pulled off her sunglasses and tucked them in her bag, putting some distance between her and this big bear of a man. "My father's the same way during salmon season."

"Is he?"

"Uh-huh. Flies up to British Columbia every year with his buddies to stand knee-deep in frigid water in hip-high boots. Never understood it, myself."

"It's a battle with the elements. You know. Man against beast. Man against nature."

"Man against pneumonia."

His blue eyes twinkled. "Hooking a fish, you get a sense of self-sufficiency that you just can't get paper-pushing."

"Yeah, a real struggle—a two-hundred pound man with hundreds of years of metallurgy and plastics behind him, against a fifteen-pound fish."

"C'mon, Casey. You've covered daredevils before. You should understand the mentality."

"I've covered them. I haven't always made sense of them. I know there's some kind of adrenaline rush involved with...danger." She wandered deeper into the cabin. They were straying into dangerous territory again, and she was determined to keep things all business. "I'm simply not genetically equipped," she explained, shrugging. "It's a male thing."

"Doesn't have to be."

Dylan flipped on a switch. Light flooded from a lamp swinging above the dining-room table. Neat piles of papers and books lay on the battered wide planks. He searched among them, then tugged a laminated photocopy out of a pile.

"You've got all the physical equipment you need for this trip, Casey. Two arms, a young back, and two legs."

His gaze flickered to her legs for the hundredth time. She resisted the urge to rub one leg up the other, to check to see if the hose she wore had caught on splinters.

Instead, she snapped the document out of his hands and concentrated on it. "What's this?"

"The map of the trip we're making."

She eyed him for using the "we" again, but his grin only widened. He came around her to stand just at her side. She sensed the heat of him against her shoulder, bare now without her jacket. She wore only a peach-colored silk shell and right now it felt as thin as tissue paper against her skin.

"This map was originally made in about 1670, probably 1672, by a French-Canadian fur trapper named Henri Duchamp."

He reached across to trace one of the lines, and his bare forearm brushed hers. She tightened her grip on the map.

"By law, old Henry could only sell his furs to the French government—and the Quebec officials took a pretty big bite. So, being a free-market kind of guy, he mapped a way to get his furs to the English and the Dutch at Fort Orange and Albany, who always paid a better price and didn't ask for a cut." Dylan traced one of the lines with his finger. His skin gleamed with a full summer's tan. The hairs on the back of his hand had been bleached fair by the sun. "Of course," he added, letting his hand drop to his side, "back then, that was treason."

"Treason," she murmured, wishing he would move back about six miles.

"Yeah, but the fur traders weren't much for loyalty—not then, anyway. They did what they damn well pleased."

"I see."

Seven miles would be better. Why was he breathing on her neck like that?

"This," she said, rattling the paper, "looks deceptively simple. Where's the catch?"

"Ah, the wary reporter." He tugged the map out of her grip and tossed it on the table. He snapped open another map, a larger one, of northern New York State. "That map *is* deceptively simple. It corresponds, somehow, to this."

Reluctantly, Casey walked to his side and glanced at the new map—a veritable anatomy of blue veins on a green background—a tangled web of rivers and ponds and lakes. A man could lose himself amid that mess for months. So could a man and a woman. Alone in the wilderness, with nothing but the stars for a roof. As intimate as Adam and Eve.

"So," she said, sharply, "good old Henry left out a few things on his map."

"There's a question whether he ever made the trip," Dylan admitted. "Or if he simply drew the map and made a bundle of wampum off selling it before fleeing west to join his Chippewa wife. After that, he disappeared into the wilderness, and from historical record."

"So," she said, leaning her hip into the table, "you're trying to prove that the trip can be made."

"Yes," he replied, fingering the laminated map. "With no more guidance than old Henry's scribbling."

She eyed him. The light fell upon his chest and left his face in dimness. Yet his eyes were alight.

"It is," she conceded, "an interesting academic question."

"Uh-huh."

"It's no wonder the alliance funded you for it."

"Uh-huh."

"So what are you leaving out, MacCabe?"

He gave her the kind of sheepish look one of his students would probably give him while explaining lost homework. "I guess I'm not going to put anything over on you, am I, Casey Starr, crack reporter?"

"Not if you hope to get me to join you."

"Well, there is a lot more," he admitted. "There are a hundred details. But nothing more I could tell you would make the journey any more dangerous, or any less exciting. This project really is as simple as it seems."

He kept staring at her, an intense, disquieting stare. She crossed her arms, wondering why she was getting goose pimples in the middle of summer. This was crazy. How had he lured her into this cabin? She had no intention of making this trip. She had no intention of camping out in the wilderness with this man.

Camping out in the wilderness. Finding their way on old historic fur-trading routes. Her, Casey Michaels, who used to get lost riding around her own hometown.

"White water," she said, as if she'd just remembered the words. "There's white water, isn't there?"

"If you've done part of the Snake River, then there's nothing up here you can't handle."

Sure there was. A six-foot, bronzed god of a man looking at her, looking through her, looking as if he would block the doorway if she tried to escape.

"What's the verdict, Casey?" he asked, leaning over to catch her eye. "I need to know. My success or failure depends on you."

She turned away from him. She shouldn't even be thinking about this. She shouldn't even be considering this.

Think sensibly. Three weeks, she thought. Three weeks without hotel bills, food bills, gas bills. Her funds were running dangerously low, and there was no other assignment on her schedule until the second week of September. She would have to scramble to find something to take the place of this one.

Of course, she had promised to stay with her sister. Her sister, with the cozy Connecticut home, with the loving husband, and the two adorable towheaded daughters... Casey hadn't seen them in over two years. She had promised that *this* year she wouldn't disappoint them. That she would stay at their house for two weeks, living inside someone else's domestic bliss, and allow herself to be set up for blind dates with Joe the carpenter and Harry the musician, who her sister claimed were *perfect* for her.

Two weeks of remembering what might have been, if her own life had not taken an abrupt turn.

She sensed Dylan's heated gaze upon her. A familiar sensation rushed through her—the same feeling she'd had when she'd first left her hometown with all her life's belongings crammed into her minivan and headed out on that wide stretch of Highway 80. It was a mishmash of sensations: a tingle of fear, a gushing surge of adrenaline....

She took a deep, deep breath.

"I'm no Girl Scout, Dylan. I might be more of a liability than a partner. But if you are sure you have no other choice," she said, turning to a blur of a smile and a sharp laugh of triumph, "then I'll consider— Oh!"

He seized her by the waist and hefted her clear off the floor. The room spun in a whirl of color and light. She grasped his shoulders for balance. Her hair swung in her face, blinding her, and through its curtain she felt, suddenly, the hard rasp of an ill-shaven cheek against her face.

Then his lips. Warm and hard. Fitting over her own mouth with a simple sureness that lacked only the click of a lock and key. She held her breath on it. The world went still. He stopped twirling her. Her mind froze. Her heart faltered on a beat. His fingers curled deep into her waist, her body flattened against his chest.

Oh...my.

Strong. He was strong. Wide shoulders, thick under her hands. He was so big against her—all throbbing, vital man. She felt oddly fragile, lifted as if she weighed no more than a flea. His hair, damp from exertion, smelled of open air and wood fires....

He broke the kiss and set her down. Her feet jarred against the floor. Her hair swung out of her eyes soon enough for her to see him take a big step back and stare at her, his grin wider than ever and his eyes twinkling with nothing less than raw, unadulterated victory.

She scraped hair off her mouth, and brushed her cheek with her fingers long after she'd tucked the last tress behind her ear. How long had it been? Certainly a simple kiss had never knocked her senseless like that before. Maybe her sister was right. It had been too long since she'd been with a man.

"Did you check into a hotel yet, Casey? Or did you come straight here?"

"Hotel?" She blinked at him as he strode clear across the cabin to the front door. The kiss obviously hadn't thrown *him.* "No. No, I came straight here."

"Good. Then let's get your things." He stretched open the cabin door for her. "You can stay in the bedroom until the launch and I'll sleep on the couch."

She threw up her hand. "Hold it, MacCabe—"

"Casey, you're going to be sharing a bedroom under the stars with me for three weeks." He flashed that all-American grin. "Don't you think we'd best get better acquainted?"

3

DYLAN HAD NEVER KNOWN a woman who could wear brown lipstick and get away with it.

Of course, the lipstick was all but kissed off now. He could still taste its residue in his mouth.

Sweet and spicy and slick.

He pressed the door of the cabin full open. *Stop it, Dylan.* Hell, if he had any sense left in him, he would put all lurid thoughts of Casey Michaels right out of his mind. The lady had BACK OFF written all over her—in bold, bright, big letters. If he had any hope of redeeming himself from that impulsive blunder, he'd best do it now—and quickly.

"The nearest hotel is fifteen miles away," he explained, stepping out into the sunshine. "And we've got a lot of work to do before the launch. Canoeing, portaging, background, orienting—do you have a bathing suit?"

"Yes."

"Good. We'll go out on the lake this afternoon, since the weather is holding." He tried his most sincere, his most encouraging smile—the kind he used when talking troubled teenagers into memorizing the Declaration of Independence. "C'mon, let's get you settled. You'll be a crack canoeist by sundown."

The smile worked. She floated across the cabin toward him, the light gleaming off the thin gold chain draped across her neck, sheening the tiny pearls in her ears. One neat, chestnut-colored brow arched above the rim of her sunglasses. She brushed by him. Dylan fixed the smile on his face and pretended not to notice the smell of her perfume as he drifted after her.

She paused to dig into her briefcase for keys. To avoid eyeing the sleek curve of those legs, he eyed her van instead. Dents marred the body, and rust had set in along the edge of the chassis. Judging by the haze of soot covering the white paint, it hadn't seen a wash in weeks. Somehow, he had expected something different for this lady. Something small and sporty and Italian.

She seized her keys, then dipped down to open the back. The hatch flew up and magazines tumbled from on high, veered off her thighs and splattered to the ground in a flap of glossy pages. She caught the top of an overstuffed duffel bag as it careened out of its niche between the wall of the van and a box, and then she lurched for a toppling pile of books.

He dipped under the shade of the hatch and helped her halt the avalanche of books. He eyed the rest of the van's contents for instability as they kept the avalanche at bay.

The van lacked a rear bench. The space where it would have been was packed with boxes and bags and suitcases, books and magazines, a scattering of empty chip bags, and a faded cup, still sticky with soda, from a fast-food restaurant.

"It was a bumpy ride to the cabin." She sidled him a glance as she shoved the duffel bag back into its niche. "Must have dislodged everything."

"Hmm," he said, lurching the books up into a manageable pile. "Nice place you've got here."

"Hey, it's home."

Apparently so. Well lived in. And by the way she expertly rifled through a large duffel bag, then plucked out a smaller case from beneath, she had lived in it for quite a while.

He thought of his own house in Bridgewater—the living room his first wife had decorated, with the white couches and the champagne-colored carpet, the glass and chrome the cleaning lady kept to shiny perfection twice a month, even in his absence.

He crouched down to pick up the fallen magazines. *American Backroads, Mountaineering, Hiking, America West, Canadian Travel, Kayaking.* Dozens of them, stuck with yellow sticky notes and scribbled in illegible shorthand. The covers sported pictures of pumped-up men frozen in mid-air poses.

He rose to his feet with a fistful of them. "Are these for work or pleasure?"

She glanced at the glossy magazines in his hands. "Work. I've got a piece in each one of them."

"You've been one busy lady." He eyed the teetering pile of magazines she'd shoved back atop one of the boxes. "I'd like to read them."

"Checking out my professional qualifications, MacCabe? A little late for that, don't you think?"

"It's never too late, Casey."

"Go ahead. Read them."

He intended to. He would read them closely and carefully, and see what the words revealed of the woman he would be spending the next three weeks with in the wilderness.

She loosed a bag from beneath a box. "This is all I need."

He grabbed the bag and slung it over his shoulder, then wadded the magazines under his elbow. She veered away from the van to close the hatch. He caught sight of a tiny swatch of yellow wadded in her hand—a piece of cloth that looked suspiciously like a bathing suit.

Hell.

He swiveled in the crackle of dried pine needles and headed toward the cabin. He would be damned if he would struggle with misgivings now. She'd agreed to join him. Yeah, it would have been a hell of a lot easier if she were good old belching Danny-boy. It would have been a hell of a lot easier to sleep next to her if she were mousy and round and didn't smell like sunshine. But he was a grown man who had had two wives in his life, and knew better than to fall for another slick-dressing working girl like Casey Michaels.

"If we're going to do this, Dylan," she said, her footsteps quick and sure behind him, "then I'll sleep on the couch. I'm not going to put you out of your own bedroom."

"House rules." He shouldered the door open and strode across the living room, toward the door beside the fireplace. "My mother taught me always to give the guests the best room. Besides," he said, hazarding a smirk at her, "you'll have plenty of time to get used to a lack of privacy when we're on the trail."

He slung her bag off his shoulder and dumped it on the bed. At the end of the bed, his athletic bag sagged open, revealing a glimpse of rolled-up clothing and his practical white underwear. He clutched the handles of the bag and shoved it closed.

"Indoor plumbing," he said, gesturing to the door on the other side of the bed. "We have to share it—it's the only one in the cabin."

That brow fluttered upward. "How decadent."

"Enjoy it while you can."

He watched as she eyed the small room. The walls bore no dead stuffed fish, only a few sconces filled with dried flowers on either side of a dreamy Impressionist print. The bedside table was covered with a lace-edged cloth and the lamp's ceramic base was painted with rosebuds. All his mother's touches. This was the only room she had been able to claim.

Casey eyed the bed, then slipped off her sunglasses. "Your bed is made."

"Yeah?"

"You make your own bed," she asked, "when you're not expecting company?"

"I'm paper-trained, too."

He hiked his hands to his hips. So he made his own bed, what was the big deal? Army Reserve training.

She avoided his eye, though he thought he glimpsed a twitch of a smile on those soft, full lips. She hazarded a glance at his closet. The mirrored panel stood open, revealing a few empty hangers, a starched shirt still in its plastic, and a pair of dress pants he'd brought on the off chance of photo opportunities with the local media.

"I just finished a horror novel," she mused, tossing her glasses upon the bed, "where the villain liked to line up his ties according to design, and his shoes according to color."

He hefted up his athletic bag. "It's late to be checking if I'm a serial killer."

"Maybe."

"Have I passed the test?"

"No ties." She shrugged, waving a hand at his closet. "No dress shoes, either."

"Later I'll let you go through my underwear drawer."

He wanted to kick himself the moment the words left his mouth. She froze. Those amber eyes widened. And every line of her sleek, lean body stiffened.

The BACK OFF signs were up again, blinking red, and it was his own damned fault. What, was he on some kind of self-destructive binge, here? He had success caught like a bird in his hand, and he had the strangest urge to open his fingers and let it go.

"Go away, MacCabe." She swung her briefcase upon the bed and gave him her shoulder. "In the next three weeks I'm going to have nothing but trees to hide behind. Now, if you don't mind, I'll take advantage of the privacy."

"I'll meet you out front."

Dylan shoved his pack just outside the door and strode straight for the back door. *C'mon, Dylan,* he told himself as he shouldered the door open and headed for the small shed in the woods. *You've always been a sucker for those designer-clothes types—all soft silks and linens and delicate gold jewelry glistening at their throats.... But you know that's not the kind of woman for you.*

And why he was thinking in these terms when he'd just met the woman and all but strong-armed her into joining him on this trek was beyond all comprehension. It was going to be a long three weeks if he had to battle his libido all the way through. He had to keep his mind on his mission. He should be grateful to her for saving his sorry little adventure from ruin.

Twenty minutes later, Dylan was securing the last bungee tie across the canoe lying atop his Jeep. Then he tugged on all the ropes to make sure the vessel was secure. He heard the slap of the screen door and Casey's light footsteps.

She stopped and said, "Why are we taking that canoe, and not the one you showed me out back?"

He glanced across the hood of the car and nearly yanked the bungee cord he was fixing right off the roof.

Gone was the sleekly-hosed glamour girl who had stridden across his backyard in high heels an hour ago. She wore an oversize yellow T-shirt and a pair of yellow-rimmed sunglasses to match. On her feet were canvas sneakers splattered with yellow daisies.

She looked about seventeen. She looked like a lemon drop, cool and tart and good enough to lick.

And he'd damned well better get those thoughts right out of his head, for there was no mistaking the don't-you-dare-touch-me look in her eyes, even if she did hide them—still—behind sunglasses.

"I just applied the last coat of pitch to the bottom of the other canoe," he explained, shoving the paddles into the back of the Jeep. "It needs at least a day to dry. This aluminum one is good enough for teaching purposes."

He rounded the car. Her T-shirt ended mid-thigh. Her legs were long and sleek and strong, but those damned lips, covered with a fresh coat of brown lipstick, looked soft enough to bruise.

"Come on," he said, opening the Jeep door for her. "There's a pond up the road a bit. Calm water. It'll be a good place to practice some strokes."

She rounded him to slide those long legs into the seat. He slammed the door on her and on his thoughts.

At least, he tried. But as soon as he slid into the driver's side he could smell her perfume—a lemony scent. Grassy. Strangely innocent. Like the kiss they'd shared in the kitchen. Powerful in its innocence, powerful in its surprise.

He gunned the motor and backed out of the clearing, then heard a rustling and the click of a pen.

"So," she said, twisting in her seat, "do you want to tell me how you came up with this idea?"

He glanced over at her. She had hiked a knee up and was using it as a table for a small yellow pad. Her T-shirt slid down to her hips, and he caught a glimpse of a matching yellow bathing suit fitting snugly to her rounded little bottom.

"I thought," he said, forcing his gaze back to the road, "that all reporters used tape recorders."

"I do. But I'm out of batteries. I'll need to go into town to-morrow to pick up them and some film and a few other things." She tapped the pen on the yellow pad. "I assume that town I passed through in a blink of an eye has an auto-matic teller machine?"

He managed a grin. "That town even has a pizza parlor, with a video game in the back." He cocked his head at her. "I assume this means you have a bank account?"

"Of course I do. What do you think, I stash my earnings in my van?"

"It'd be a great archaeological project to go digging through that van."

"Don't get any ideas."

"And if you have a bank account, that usually means you have a home. Somewhere."

She frowned at him. She ran her fingers through her cap of chocolate brown hair, and the silken strands of it slipped neatly back into place. "Still digging, MacCabe? I'm sup-posed to be the one asking *you* the questions, remember?"

"You're dodging."

"What do you expect? That I'll admit to having an off-shore bank account in the Cayman Islands?"

"Right about now," he murmured, eyeing the spangle of yellow daisies on her sneakers, "I wouldn't be surprised by anything you say, Casey Michaels."

The muscle in her calf flexed, her neck tightened. "If you must know, I do have a home. It's Morristown, New Jersey. And it's you who are dodging."

"New Jersey, huh?"

"Yes, and no Jersey jokes, you hear? So," she said, click-ing her pen three times, "where did you get the idea for this trek?"

Persistent, he thought. That was good. She would need persistence if she was going to finish this trip with him.

"First things first, Casey." The tires crunched on gravel as he turned into a clearing just before the banks of a pond. The bank had been leveled for use as a launch for small craft. "We'll set the boat out here. You'll have plenty of time to ask me questions later, but we only have a few more hours of sun to teach you the fine art of canoeing."

"C'mon, MacCabe, we're talking about paddling a long, narrow boat across still water." She tucked the pen and pad back into her bag. "It can't be all that difficult." She eyed him above the rim of her sunglasses. "Don't tell me you're one of those enthusiasts who is a stickler for form, and has a mouthful of jargon for every lesson?"

"Nope." He reached behind her chair and shoved an orange vest into her hands. "Don't forget your PFD."

"It's a life vest." She picked it up with two fingers. The color had long ago faded to a muddy shade of orange. "I can swim."

"House rules, remember? It's the law." He shoved the door open. "Now help me unload this technocraft by grabbing it by the gunwales and sliding it to the stern."

One fine, smooth dark eyebrow arched above the yellow sunglasses. He grinned at her through the cab of the Jeep as he snapped the first bungee cord free. Her lips twitched in a smile — a soft thing, hesitant, strangely sweet.

Oh, boy, Dylan. He ducked behind the Jeep to snap free the last ties. *Steady, boy. Steady.*

He gripped the canoe and slid it off the back of the Jeep, then dipped under it to settle the mid-slat upon his shoulders and stretch the tumpline across his forehead. He carried it like that to the launch, kicking off his flip-flops before splashing in at the edge.

He turned around just in time to see her pull the T-shirt over her head.

For the split second her face was covered, he took a good

straight look at the body he would be sleeping under the stars with for the next three weeks. *Legs.* Long, long legs, emphasized by the high cut of her yellow checked bathing suit. Lean, lean, lean—beyond slim, almost to the point of skinny. Her nipples beaded against the suit, though the day was warm and windless, and as she lowered her arms he realized that while her breasts were small, they were exquisitely shaped. Heavy-bottomed. Tip-tilted.

Thank God he'd chosen to wear his boxy bathing suit, rather than the tight-fitting briefs he preferred in the water. Maybe he should rethink what he'd packed for the trip.

Scraping the canoe secure in the gravel, he rounded the Jeep to grab the paddles and muscle into his own life preserver.

"MacCabe, what is this, some sort of knot test?"

She stood with her hands on her hips, the life preserver hanging off her neck, the ties on either side sagging.

"That's Danny's preserver. He's of—ah—wider proportions than you."

"And he ties his knots like a sailor."

"I'll help you."

She lifted one arm out of the way as he plucked at the ties at the level of her breasts. He smelled that scent again, rising from her hair—lemon and green cut grass. His fingers fumbled with the ties.

She had smooth, smooth skin. No moles, no freckles, and tanned to an even gold. She'd shoved her sunglasses atop her head, and so when she glanced up at him he finally got a good look at her eyes. Light brown. Light brown with sparks of gold.

Young. So very young. She couldn't be thirty. And here he was, looking down the barrel at forty and feeling like some sort of prehistoric fly stuck in those amber eyes.

Too young. Yeah, that was the problem, he told himself. She was too young for him.

"We're not really going to wear these," she said, finding sudden interest in the fumbling of his fingers, "during the whole trip?"

"Of course we are." Good, one set of ties free. He swiftly knotted them so the vest fit more snugly. "It's water-safety rules, you know."

"Are we going to need them?"

"You can never be too safe."

"That's not the answer to my question."

He rounded her to work on the other set of ties, under the other arm. "If you can swim, probably not."

"Probably."

"Mm-hmm."

"MacCabe, you realize I'm not going anywhere with you unless I get the full story."

"Oh, you'll get it." He finished tying, and swept a paddle up from the ground. He shoved it into her hands. "First things first."

He splashed knee-deep into the water and clattered his paddle into the canoe. The water felt good and cold on his bare legs. If he was lucky, it would be good and cold all along the route they were taking.

He held the gunwales of the canoe as she kicked off her sneakers and followed him. "Climb in. Carefully," he warned. "An empty canoe wobbles."

She grasped the edge and sank a foot into the canoe. Her knuckles whitened as she shifted her weight. The canoe heaved in his grip. Her eyes widened. Gingerly, she transferred her weight and swung her other leg over the side.

He heard her gasp as he pushed off and swung his own weight into the canoe.

"It won't be so unsteady in the other canoe," he explained. "The other canoe will be weighted with our gear."

"Uh-huh."

"Now, listen," he said, focusing on the lesson ahead, as he dipped the paddle in and shot them out into open water. "There're a lot of different ways to paddle...."

He taught with his back to her, twisting around to watch her progress now and again, leaning across the canoe to adjust the position of her hands on the paddle, or to illustrate how to get the most push out of the stroke. She listened with all the attentiveness of a National Honor Student. Quiet, studious, intent. Determined.

She did well. She had endurance. But after a few hours he sensed the flagging of her energy in the sluggishness of her stroke. She lacked the upper-body strength needed to propel a canoe for the full duration of a summer's day. He wondered, again, if he hadn't made a colossal mistake, egging this woman on to take his challenge.

Why had he done it, anyway? He had all but come to terms with the fact that the trek would have to be canceled. Danny-boy had made sure of that. Dylan had already been planning to return the grant to the geographical alliance, with hopes of winning it again next year. Next summer. With a partner less likely to cause the same kind of trouble—a partner who was most definitely not a long-legged amber-eyed beauty, either.

But giving up the trip meant four weeks before returning to work, and no plans. Four weeks of hanging around Flynn's pub and water-skiing or fishing on the weekends at the cabin. He'd had his fill of that in July, knowing he would be off doing something more exciting in August. He'd spent his whole year planning for the four weeks in August when he would do something that would prove he hadn't turned into his own moniker in Bridgewater—Dull-as-Dishwater-Dylan.

Then she had waltzed into his backyard looking all sleek and breezy and worldly. He was a sucker, for sure, to fall for the same kind of woman every time.

"I think you've got it," he said, as they reached a narrow in the pond. "Let's do something different—I've got to teach you how to ferry."

Uses different muscles, he thought, as he took a break to explain how they were going to sidle the canoe from one bank to the other without any forward motion. Of course, there was only the faintest of currents in this neck of the pond. Not like some of the fast-moving rivers they would be navigating, the hairpin curves littered with boulders they would have to ferry across, to avoid white water and mishaps. But that wasn't till the second half of the trip, when, hopefully, she would be better conditioned.

He glanced over his shoulder. She dug the paddle into the water. She'd bitten off most of that brown lipstick, and sweat gleamed in the hollow of her throat.

Her legs were braced in the bottom of the boat, her toes curling into the ribs, her thighs taut, the yellow-checked bathing suit collapsing into ripples over her abdomen.

Hell. His paddle clattered as he dropped it into the canoe and held his hand out for hers.

"What?"

"Secure the paddle. Under the struts."

"Why?" she asked, as she did as she was told.

"Time for lesson number three, Casey."

With one well-timed push, he heaved the canoe over and deposited them both into a cold bath.

She sputtered up from the water and shoved her hair off her face. "All right, I get it, you're one of those sadistic football coaches, right?" She checked for her sunglasses, still hanging around her neck. "I had a gym teacher like you in sixth grade. Took pleasure in her students' pain. Well, are you satisfied, Dylan?"

No. He trod water. The cold eased his torment somewhat, but he sensed that the only real ease he would get was hot, and it lay between her long, lean legs.

"C'mon, Casey. The water's fine."

"For penguins, maybe." She swam over to where the overturned canoe drifted. "Now, are you going to tell me how we get back into this thing?"

"Lesson number three. Bring it to the shore, if you can."

She started paddling toward the shore, but he seized one of her legs—hard and lean and slippery in his hand. She narrowed her eyes at him. Her chocolate brown hair lay slicked back against her head, and instead of looking unkempt and sodden, she looked like one of those models in the mascara commercials—lipstick all but intact, droplets careening picturesquely over her cheeks.

"Uh-uh. That's the easy way, Casey. We're going to learn the hard way."

"Of course." She twisted her lips at him. "Is it sergeant? Or lieutenant-major?"

"It's Dylan to you."

"Not Sir Dylan, that's for sure. Chivalry is obviously dead in this neck of the woods."

"Move toward the shore," he said, "until you can feel the bottom."

He paddled in her wake, one hand gripping the canoe, until she hesitated and rose up breast-high in the water.

"All right," she said, swiping both hands over her face. The water lapped at the knotted peaks of her breasts. "Now what?"

"You're the lighter one." He pushed the canoe so she

stood midship. "Pull yourself up and over the gunwale at the center, here. I'll hold it as still as I can."

Two attempts failed. She gave him a look out of the corner of her eye. On the third attempt, she got high enough for the gunwale of the boat to dig into her belly. She bent in two, then struggled to hike her legs into the canoe.

There it was, that tight little bottom with the elastic edge of her yellow-checked bathing suit clinging to the curve. Her legs flailed as she tried to pull herself in. He stared at her, trying to hold the canoe still, while erotic visions flooded his mind.

Finally, he shoved the heel of his hand against her bottom—felt the give of flesh, felt the heat of her—and he lurched her into the boat.

She struggled to a sitting position in the wobbling vessel and gave him a look over the gunwale that could have burned a hole through glass.

"I think," she said, "you're enjoying this."

"What," he retorted, pulling himself into the canoe, "is there not to enjoy?"

He seized his paddle and fixed his gaze on an outcropping on the other side of the pond, then dug the blade into the water.

Think of the journey, he told himself, as the wind of their motion chilled his skin. Three long weeks with the image of that tight little ass in his head.

Heck. He should have known better.

But he had a feeling this trip was going to be one hell of an adventure.

4

"THE SHOWER IS ALL yours."

Casey bolted upright on the couch. She shook herself from an exhausted haze in time to see Dylan saunter out of the cabin's only bedroom. She fumbled for the paperback splayed on the couch, and in her awkwardness sent it flying over the edge with a flap of yellowed pages. She hazarded a glance at Dylan. He'd rounded the counter, stuck his head into the refrigerator and hadn't spared her a glance.

She retrieved the book and laid it back on the pine-board coffee table. She eased herself to her feet, wincing at the ache in her shoulders. When they'd returned from the pond, she had insisted that Dylan take the first shower, claiming she had to unload some luggage from the back of her van. The truth of the matter was that she was too exhausted to make any effort, even the effort to take a shower. All she wanted to do was collapse in a soft bed and sleep.

But she didn't want Dylan to see that. Not after the past few hours at the pond. He'd acted strangely. Of course, she didn't know him well enough to judge, but it seemed to her he'd lost some of the forceful enthusiasm that had bowled her over and led her into agreeing to join him on this trip. Or maybe he'd just been playing the part of football coach, and she'd come up short of expectations.

"How 'bout burgers for dinner?"

Casey jerked at the sound of his voice. She glanced up to see him peering at her over the refrigerator door.

"That's about all we've got," he said, straightening. "Burgers and beer. Unless you want to go into town—"

"No." The thought of bouncing over rutted roads for fifteen miles was enough to send her screaming back into the canoe. "No, burgers will be fine. I'll be out in a few minutes to help."

She winced and grimaced all the way to the bedroom. She closed the door behind her, stripped off her T-shirt and bathing suit, then headed toward the bathroom.

She halted at the door. She stared wide-eyed into the small room. Mist billowed in the air. Steam fogged the mirror. A towel lay damp across the tiled floor. Brown bristles speckled the white porcelain sink. The scent of aftershave floated on the air. The shower curtain was swept halfway open, as if Dylan had just stepped dripping wet and naked out of the tub.

She let her hands drift up from her elbows to her shoulders, to protect her naked breasts from the caress of the settling steam. The last lingering tendrils of her exhaustion receded like mist under a hot sun. Suddenly she was tinglingly, shockingly awake.

Trust a man, she thought, to leave a bathroom in such a state. The toilet seat stood shamelessly upright. A razor lay by the side of the sink, smeared with cream. The tube of toothpaste lay abandoned, squeezed tight in the middle. A damp towel lay halfway over the dowel behind the shower.

C'mon, Casey, get a grip. She was used to the sterile uniformity of hotel bathrooms—the crinkling white strip of paper across the toilet, the palm-size bars of soap. She was used to seeing one toothbrush dangling above the sink. She had forgotten what it was like to share a bathroom with a man.

Shaking herself, she stepped resolutely into the tub. Into

a small, warm puddle of water. Trying all the while to ignore the fact that this water had recently sluiced off his skin. She reached down and cranked the knob to Cold.

She scrubbed herself clean. She let the cold water shiver over her skin and strip off the sheen of soap. She showered fast and hard, and when it was done, she wrapped herself in a towel and stood staring into the same mirror he'd used to shave, feeling edgy and completely unlike herself, wondering how she was going to handle the intimacies of the trip they were going to take if she felt so unbalanced after doing something as simple as sharing a canoe and a bathroom.

She yanked the towel off her body and let it drop to the floor, then padded into the neutrality of the bedroom. Her rucksack lay open on the bed and she rifled through it until she found fresh undergarments. She put them on and was about to pull a cotton T-shirt and shorts out of her bag when something soft and silky brushed her knuckles. She paused, then pulled on the cloth. A little slip of a silk dress poured out onto the bed.

Casey swept it up and held the scooped neckline against her chest. The silk felt cool and soft against her skin.

She remembered buying this dress. She'd purchased it two years ago. Two years ago, after she'd received the settlement—the money that was supposed to compensate her for her husband's sudden death. She remembered carrying the check around with her for days, even bringing it uncashed to her therapy session to show it to Jillian. She remembered spending hours touching it, fingering it, looking at the number printed in black ink and trying to reconcile it to all that she'd lost. She'd wondered, aloud, what she should do with all that money. She asked Jillian the same.

Jillian, as cool as ice, had lit a cigarette and sat back in her creaking leather chair and suggested that Casey blow it all.

Or part of it, at least. Do something mad. Fly to Paris. Buy a sports car. Eat at the fanciest restaurant in Manhattan. Buy Tiffany diamonds.

Casey had mused for days, then, in an uncharacteristic spurt of spontaneity, had gone out and spent a good chunk of the money on clothing—linen suits and chic little dresses and shoes that matched them, with all the scarves and accessories she could ever desire. She'd bought the kind of clothes she had no use for, and never would have bought in all the years before. Then she'd spent a day at a salon getting her long, straight hair cut in the style she still wore, and watching a makeup artist wield his magic upon her face.

After those crazy few days, Casey had looked at herself in the mirror and seen a woman she didn't recognize: a stylish young woman. And she'd begun to think that she *could* start a new life—if she had the courage. Which, it turned out, was what Jillian had intended for her to realize in the first place....

She hugged the silk dress close to her skin. She had changed. Oh, yes, her life had changed. But sometimes...sometimes she felt a little too much like the scared young woman from New Jersey who had put on pretty clothes and brown lipstick and set off with a hope and a prayer on Route 80 West.

She snapped the dress free of wrinkles and wrestled it over her head.

"So," Casey said, as she stepped out of the bedroom a few minutes later, "how are those burgers coming?"

"I only just fired up the grill," he said. "Had to change a propane tank."

He glanced up at her. He paused in shaking pepper over a plate of burger patties. His gaze swept from her wet, brushed-back hair to the strappy flat sandals on her feet.

A tingling tremor skittered up her spine—a strange fluttery sensation she couldn't quite define. Uniquely feminine. Completely unnerving.

He started shaking pepper again. She pushed one of the stools aside and leaned into the counter. The dress wasn't inappropriate, she told herself. Maybe a little sassy for the Adirondacks, but not out of line for a barbecue. She gestured toward the plate of raw hamburger patties in front of him—huge pink patties that he was still sprinkling with pepper. "Those look good."

"My one and only specialty."

"Any chance of a salad to go along with those hunks of cow?"

"Ahh..."

She narrowed her eyes at him. "No chance you and Danny-boy bought any lettuce, hmm?"

"There might be some tomatoes in the fridge." He put the pepper on the counter, then backed off with the plate of burgers in his hand. "Feel free to dig around."

He shouldered his way out the back door. She rounded the counter, pulled the fridge open and frowned. Dylan wasn't kidding. But for a half gallon of milk, some eggs, and mounds of hamburger buns, the refrigerator yielded up no viable side-dish for dinner. She grabbed a beer and popped the cap, then started opening cabinets as she took the first shocking swig. She'd never been much of a beer drinker, but over the past years she'd found it helped in "bonding" with the guys she was writing about if she could drink the drink and talk the talk.

Not that she wanted to bond with Dylan, of course, on anything but the most professional level. She simply wanted him to see her as just one of the boys. Just a substitute for "Danny-boy."

Sure, Casey, that's why you wore this dress.

She shook the thought out of her head and set her mind

resolutely on dinner. She poked her way through the bare cabinets, but found nothing but mismatched coffee cups, steak sauces and canned beans. Then, in a high cabinet, she stumbled on a box of pasta and a cluster of glass jars.

She heard the slap of the screen door and Dylan's sure footsteps, just as the pot of pasta she'd set on the stove started to boil.

"What's cooking?" he asked, coming up behind her.

"Pasta."

"Really?"

"Yes...it's a strange selection you have here," she said, sliding along the counter to get away from the brush of his breath on her shoulders. "Canned beans and...artichoke hearts." She reached for a jar. "Sun-dried tomatoes."

"What?"

"Don't worry, Dylan," she said, fussing with the jars so they stood evenly on the counter. "I find it charming for a man to prefer balsamic vinegar to the regular stuff."

"I didn't buy this."

"Defensiveness is a true sign of guilt."

"No, really," he said, eyeing her with a grin. "This must be leftovers. Probably from Renee."

Casey's smile froze on her face. She didn't have to ask to know that Renee was a woman. A woman that he must have brought to this cabin for an intimate dinner of pasta salad and...what else? Wine? Candlelight? Raucous love-making before a roaring fire?

"Or Janet," he added, rolling back against the counter and giving her a sly smile, "though that was too long ago and not really likely."

Had any other jock said those words to her, she would have scoffed and written it off as youthful arrogance. But Dylan stood there grinning at her with a twinkle in his eye, and she felt an odd frisson—the way women throughout the centuries must have felt when faced with a blatant, un-repentant rogue.

She arched a brow and said, "Renee and Janet are your sisters, no doubt."

"Oh, no," he said, grabbing a dishrag and wiping his hands on it. "Renee and Janet were my wives."

He had the nerve to stand there and grin at her while she absorbed this information. *Wives.* Two of them, at least. And spoken in the past tense, as if they were already gone.

Then she realized she didn't even know if he still had a wife. She had assumed not, because he wore no ring... because of the way he'd grabbed her and kissed her... because of the way he'd spoken to her...because of the way he'd molded his hand over her bottom this afternoon, as he pushed her into the canoe.

But all that didn't mean anything. He was of an age to be married. Not all men wore rings. And the wife wasn't here, if there was one. He could be as much of a modern-day roué as he looked. She'd seen uglier situations on assignment. Heck, for all she knew, those wives of his could have been disembodied and entombed in the woods. She didn't know anything at all about this man.

Except that he was handsome. Strikingly so, leaning up against the counter with his shoulders as wide as a beam, the golden rays of the late-afternoon sun pouring through the window and shining on his hair. He was grinning at her, his eyes twinkling, watching her try to get over that bombshell.

He had a disconcerting habit of doing that. Dropping bombs on her. Knocking her off her feet. Sweeping her along in his plans. She was beginning to think he did it on purpose, just to watch her reaction.

"So," she said, forcing her voice to sound casual, "should

I have checked expiration dates before I opened all these jars?"

"Naw. It was probably Renee's doing. She was here only last summer. Everything's fresh enough."

Fresh, indeed. Less than a year widowed or divorced. Divorced, most likely, or else he wouldn't be making so light of the matter. Didn't that just fit—that Dylan MacCabe, log-chopping, camp-loving woodsman, would flit in and out of relationships as easily as a wild buck?

She grabbed a wooden spoon to fish a piece of rotini out of the roiling water. "Mrs. MacCabe had good taste."

"Both of them did. They married me, didn't they?" He twisted a bottle of black olives around so he could see the label. "Of course, they both dumped me, too."

He plucked an olive out of the colander in the sink. She busied herself blowing on the bit of purple pasta until it was cool enough to test, telling herself all the while not to ask, not to ask.

Don't ask.

Though why any woman in her right mind would dump a man like this was beyond her comprehension. Of course, divorce as a concept was totally beyond her comprehension. She'd been brought up to honor marriage as a sacred union. Sacrosanct. A bonding for life. It was the stubborn Catholic in her.

"Aren't you in the least bit curious, Casey?"

Oh, yes. She was curious. The curiosity was eating at her—she was a reporter, after all. But she knew the way the game was played. If she asked him about his wives, then that would be a wide-open invitation for him to ask her the same kinds of questions. "Your personal life is none of my business, Dylan."

"That's not what I asked. I asked if you were curious. As to why my wives dumped me."

"Hmm, let me think." She turned against the counter and pretended to muse, blowing on the pasta between thoughts. "Was it the way you threw them in the lake every time you took them out in the canoe? Or because you forced them to bait hooks with worms?" She waved the wooden spoon in the air. "Or maybe you like to hang from your feet like a bat in the middle of the night. Eat raw meat for breakfast. Chase after young women. Am I getting warm?"

A slow smile slipped up one corner of his mouth. A dangerous smile. "Not even close."

She could think of a thousand other quirks, involving exotic oils and whipped cream and bedsheets, but she didn't have the wit or the nerve to articulate them. She turned abruptly back to the stove. "Maybe you just have bad judgment." She slipped the cool rotini between her lips, then bit it to see if it was done. "In any case, I'm not here," she said, tossing the hard rotini into the sink, "to find out about your personal life, Mr. MacCabe."

"Back to that, are we?"

"What?"

"'Mr. MacCabe.' You say it like you're pushing me about a mile away."

"I'm trying to tell you," she said, stirring the pot a little too viciously, "that you should be careful what you confess." She'd used this tactic before, to ward off personal questions. "We're going to be partners on this journey, but in the end, I'm a reporter, MacCabe. I'll use whatever I need, whatever you tell me, if it has an impact on the story I'm going to write."

"Ah, Casey, promise you'll paint me as a wild man."

"I'm not kidding."

"Neither am I. Paint me as a cad, a monster, a defiler of fair maidens. Might spice up my life a bit." He leaned toward her. "And it's going to be a long three weeks, with only each other to talk to. Best you know my foibles now."

"Foible number one: You can't keep your own secrets. Foible number two—"

"My foibles with *women*," he corrected, eyeing another black olive. "I tend to get mixed up with the wrong type."

She arched a brow at him. There was obviously no stopping the man. "Should I get out my tape recorder, Dylan? Or a book on Freud?"

"Janet and I met in high school," he continued, popping another olive into his mouth. "She was the homecoming queen and was well on her way to managing a restaurant when she dumped me."

"Homecoming queen, huh?" She could imagine the type. Blond. Cheerleader. Long legs. She sank her teeth into a piece of green rotini. It tasted strangely bitter.

"I was a high-school football hero," he explained, grinning. "Make sure that gets into the article, will you?"

"I'll have to check the facts first."

"First-string quarterback. Two years in a row. Made the regional finals, my senior year." He sank an elbow onto the counter and leaned into it. "Wife number two—Renee— worked for a children's book publisher in the city. She's back there now."

"They sound like terribly dangerous women, MacCabe. Terrible, wicked temptresses."

"I can't help myself," he said, with an exaggerated sigh. "It's purely hormonal. I'm attracted to strong women. Real independent types." He paused on a breath. "Women who wear silky dresses in the woods."

She jerked around to meet his gaze. Though a grin lingered upon his lips, there was something in those blue eyes, something sharp and intent and very, very serious.

A moment passed between them. A moment when Casey

realized there was no humor behind that grin, and she found herself staring into the heart of a very solid, very serious man, grappling with very weighty thoughts. An odd moment. So odd, she stood still and blinked, wondering if she was imagining the sudden shift in the conversation, wondering if she was just imagining the silent communication between them. A brief-but-unmistakable acknowledgment of a pure sexual attraction. A swift but silent acknowledgment that Dylan wasn't all that comfortable with the attraction, either.

She stood, too stunned to speak. A piece of pasta tipped off her spoon and splashed back into the boiling water. For she'd hardly come to terms with her own body's strange reactions to Dylan—and there Dylan stood, in full and open admission of a physical attraction she was not yet ready to admit to herself.

Suddenly Dylan laughed. A low, rumbling, dangerous sort of laugh that left the hair on the back of her neck prickling.

"Don't worry, Casey. You're in no danger from me." His gaze stayed fixed upon hers, bright and blue and in fierce defiance of his own words. "I've struck out twice already. After the second strike, I figured what I need is a nice hometown girl, someone with family on her mind, and little else."

"You were born a few decades too late," she said, trying to make her voice light. She turned back to the boiling pot of pasta. "They don't make women like that anymore."

"Have you ever been married, Casey?"

She stiffened. She'd known it was coming, sooner or later. Once the ice broke, once they started talking about more than business, there was no way she could dam the questions. All she could do was hold him off for as long as possible.

"I was married. Only once." She cast a glance over her shoulder, toward the screen door and the smoke billowing from the grill. "Shouldn't you check on those burgers?"

BY THE TIME CASEY went out into the backyard with a bowl of warm pasta salad in her hands, she noticed, thankfully, that Dylan had dropped the whole subject of marriage. As they ate peppery, overdone burgers off paper plates, the conversation drifted to trivial things—the relative benefits of steak sauce versus catsup, raw burgers versus medium rare, the latest horror novel by a bestselling author. Casey ate with relish—she hadn't realized how hungry she was until she sank her teeth into the meat.

The sun drifted low and cast long shadows across the ground. Dylan lit a series of candles on the table. The lemon scent of citronella billowed around them, chasing back the evening onslaught of mosquitos.

A silence fell between them. It should have been comfortable. Her belly was full and warm, six ounces of beer coursed through her veins, and a light breeze rustled the trees and brought relief from the day's heat. But the silence was tense, uncertain; like that between any two strangers thrust together at a party who had run out of things to say. The light from the kitchen poured out into the yard, reminding her that soon they would both be sleeping in close proximity in the small cabin.

Dylan settled on a lounge chair beside the picnic table. He took a swig from his beer. She could hear his throat working it down.

"Did I tell you my grandfather built this cabin with his own hands?" he said, his gaze drifting toward the building. "About seventy years ago."

"No," she said, thinking this at least was a neutral enough subject. "It looks good for its age."

"It's been fixed up a few times since," he admitted. "New windows, new roof. But back in the twenties, it was nothing but a shack. Grandpa used to make moonshine here."

She blinked at him and laughed. A nervous, abrupt laugh. Another bombshell. "Dylan...you're kidding, right?"

"No, no, it's true," he said, grinning as he toyed with his beer. "Did you notice those two big brown bottles on the mantel? Those are his moonshine jugs."

She cast him a doubtful eye.

"It's true," he protested, with a slap of his hand across his heart. "When I was kid, every summer instead of playing 'war' or 'cowboys and Indians,' we played 'Beat the excise men' and 'Get the moonshine to town.'"

She narrowed her eyes at him, struggling suddenly with the image of a little Dylan and his friends tearing wildly through the woods, laughing. And she felt an odd pang in her chest.

She took a sharp breath to force it away. "Dylan, did your grandfather have any compunction about telling impressionable kids how he broke the law?"

"He always said that a bad law is no law at all." He shrugged with a quick heave of his shoulders. "Anyway, we just figured that Grandpa was so old it was as if he lived back in the Old West, with Jesse James and Billy the Kid, when outlawing was fun."

"Your poor mother." She let her gaze drift to the darkening woods. "She must have hated those games."

"Not really. She and everyone else thought Grandpa was harmless. Full of tall tales."

She paused, eyeing him over the lip of her bottle as his words hung in the air. She spoke out of pure reporter's instinct. "But you didn't think so, did you?"

"Oh, no. I'm sure everything he told us was true, right down to the last wild detail."

"Dylan," she chided, "you are a romantic."

"I've had two wives. Of course I'm a romantic."

He smiled at her then, a wide, honest grin—the first easy communication they'd had since that tense moment in the kitchen. Casey tried not to grow warm at his glance. She really tried. She let her gaze skitter away and she took a gulp of beer. It washed down her throat as tasteless as water.

Great. Three weeks in the wilderness with a romantic. She must be losing her mind.

"Grandpa's stories were hard for any boy to resist." Dylan leaned forward in his chair, his gaze following the outline of the woods, growing more murky with the dying day. "I remember one story in particular. Grandpa told us about an Indian he'd met when he was a young man. A Seneca still living in the woods up here."

"A Seneca," she said, arching a brow higher.

"Yeah, you know. An Iroquois. C'mon, Casey, we're talking seventy years ago. There was still homesteading going on in Oklahoma." He waved a hand toward the woods. "And this land, it wasn't all fenced off as private property or relegated to national park status back then."

"Sounds like your MacCabe ancestor has kissed the Blarney stone."

"Casey," he said with mock shock, "you're *not* a romantic."

She blinked at him. The comment pricked her. She felt, strangely, like wincing. She *had* been a romantic. Once. A long time ago. She'd given up on happily-ever-afters after her husband had died.

"Call me a cynic." She took another swig from her now empty bottle and planted it with decided force upon the scarred wooden picnic table. "Do you have any idea how many wild stories I've heard in my travels?"

"No. I'd like to hear them."

"Well, we've got three weeks coming." She swung her legs over the bench, stretched them out, and leaned back against the table. "Did you ever hear about that guy who parachutes off skyscrapers? Well, I've interviewed him. I've also interviewed a man who lives in Yosemite. I mean, *lives* in Yosemite. Kills deer and hunts rabbits to eat, sleeps in a cave. I keep telling myself I'm going to write it all down someday. Call it 'Travels across America,' or 'The American Character,' or something just as highfalutin'. But I never seem to have the time." She tilted her head at him. "Sounds like your grandfather's story would fit right in with all the other tall tales."

"If you do write that book, tell the tale about the Seneca Indian," he said, settling back in his chair, "who showed my grandpa a canoe route through to Canada."

Casey stilled. A chorus of evening bugs brought their song to a sudden swell. A citronella candle sputtered and shot a curl of smoke into the air.

Well, well, well. Dylan had a method to his madness. She stared at him, but he seemed strangely reluctant to meet her eye.

"Should I get my tape recorder for this, Dylan?"

He shrugged, then twisted his bottle in his hand, over and over. "I thought you were out of batteries."

"I have an adapter," she replied, nodding to the outlet near the door to the cabin.

"I'd rather you just sat and listened." His gaze flickered to her, then back out to the woods. "Just this once."

Her fingers itched for a pad of paper and a pen. She leaned toward him, sensing a story. She watched him as he took a deep swig of his beer, then planted the empty bottle on the table. She realized with a jolt that he was finally going to admit to her the secret he'd kept since the afternoon, and that secret didn't seem to be anything as dangerous as she'd expected.

She wondered if Dylan would ever stop surprising her. She wondered if she could ever get a handle on the man, pigeonhole him, mark him for a type and then dismiss him as she'd done with so many of the men she'd written about.

"Grandpa said the Seneca showed him a canoe route into Canada," he began. He hung on to the empty beer bottle for a while, tracing patterns in the sweat on the glass. "The old Indian told him fur traders used to take it, but they always needed an Indian guide, because the Indians were the only ones who knew the signs."

"Signs?"

"Landmarks. Rock formations. Petroglyphs. All the markers that showed the way." He released the beer bottle, then folded his hands upon his flat belly and tipped back in the chair. "As a boy I used to play that my friends and I met the Indian, he showed us the route and then saved us from certain peril."

"This is too wild, Dylan."

"I thought so, too. I'd long since written off the story as just a crazy yarn to fill a boy's imagination. Everybody had. It got to the point where people were saying that Grandpa was finally senile, always insisting he was telling the truth in those bootlegging stories—and now none of his cronies were alive to back him up." He let the chair drop to the ground. "He's nearly ninety, you know. Still kicking. But half the time he isn't really here anymore. Everybody stopped believing him a long time ago."

"Except you."

She'd murmured the words. She'd not meant to say them

aloud, but they lingered between them in the soft silence of the evening.

"No," he admitted. "Even I thought he was full of blarney. I thought he should be happy knowing that he was a good storyteller, and stop insisting on everyone believing everything he said. I even told him so, once."

Casey suddenly realized that dusk had turned to twilight, and the glow from the kitchen had grown bright and golden, mimicking the flickering golden light of the citronella candles. Darkness had fallen upon them suddenly, and now it seemed to draw them together in silence.

A strange silence. An intimate silence. Nothing had changed; they still sat with an old scarred wooden table between them, yet the darkness cloaked them in intimacy.

"Then one day, about two years ago, I was in the middle of some research on early Bridgewater—my hometown— when I came across an article in the newspaper in the late 1920s about how the Adirondack creeks were considered to be one of the thoroughfares for illegal liquor coming down from Canada."

Dylan flexed his fingers and tipped farther back in his chair. He leaned his head back into the cup of his entwined fingers.

Casey watched him, riveted.

"Then," Dylan continued, "not long after, I stumbled on Henri's map—in a totally unrelated bit of research on seventeenth-century Quebec. It was eerie. And I could no longer deny that there were some mighty coincidental links here."

"Dylan...you didn't mention any of this in your grant papers, did you?"

He gave her a lopsided smile. "Fifteen years in the school system has taught me political expedience, if nothing else. Do you think the alliance would have sponsored me if they knew I was following an old moonshiner's route into Canada?"

She knew they wouldn't. It wasn't academic enough. It didn't have the smell of old parchment and ancient languages. But it had heart. Real heart. And a realization came to her—at first no more than a niggling thought, but which soon bloomed big and fragrant.

"This whole thing," she said, leaning toward him, "this whole trip...you're doing it to prove your grandfather was telling the truth."

Dylan sat in silence, his face limned by the candlelight. His lips tight, his face still.

"You are, aren't you?" She sidled up on her knees on the picnic bench. "You're going to find the water route through to Canada, not just because fur traders did it three hundred years ago, but because your grandfather claims to have done it seventy years ago."

He shrugged. He reached for his beer, curled his lips over the mouth and tipped it up, though he'd already finished the dregs. She sat back, incredulous. Her fingers itched for a pen and a pad of paper. She wanted to write this all down. Already, the story was taking shape in her head. Not the main story for *American Backroads*, but another story she would write about the man—a story about moonshine and the ingenuity of bootleggers; a story about a man in the midst of reliving a childhood adventure, setting forth to redeem an aging grandfather's honor.

She stared at him. He seemed strangely uncertain, leaning back in his chair, busying himself with knocking away a moth that had fluttered past him toward the citronella flame.

She curled a hand around one of the candleholders. The flame inside warmed the thick glass. She peered in to gaze at the yellow wax, then tipped the glass, so the pale yellow liquid poured away from the drowning wick.

"Why didn't you tell me this," she asked, easing the candle back down, "when you were first trying to convince me to join you?"

"I didn't know what kind of woman you were."

She blinked in surprise. "What does that mean?"

"Some women are swayed by the academic challenge. Others are swayed by one man's private passion."

Somewhere in the woods an owl hooted. Dylan's gaze fixed on her again, and the heat of it seeped through her body, like the heat of the glass candleholder warming the palm of her hand.

Then the intimacy that had fallen over them and had seemed so comfortable suddenly tightened, binding them by the force of their locked gazes. She began to realize the enormity of the decision she'd made this afternoon in the coolness of Dylan's cabin. By agreeing to join him on this voyage, she'd chosen to share three weeks of nights with him. Twenty-one evenings as private as this one, lit by the stars and flickers of candlelight. Twenty-one evenings of intimate discussions. Sharing thoughts. Sharing private passions.

Abruptly she stood. The picnic bench scraped against the ground. "I knew you were hiding something." Her bottle wobbled upon the table. She seized the neck to still it. "I just didn't know it was such a good story."

He replied, in a strange, soft voice, "I'm glad you think so."

"I do. And I'll use it. In my piece, I mean." She ran her fingers through her drying hair. "But now, I should be off to bed. We've got a busy day ahead of us tomorrow."

Somehow she made her way around the picnic table. Somehow she made it past him, past the hand he'd stretched out to her, past the whispered sound of her name on his lips.

Casey...

She slapped the door shut behind her and in a blind, frantic haze, made her way through to the bedroom. Dylan's bedroom. The bedroom of a bootlegger's grandson. In whose sheets she would be lying this night.

Alone.

5

CASEY HEAVED THE CLEAR morning air into her lungs as she pounded across the country path, avoiding tree roots and sharp-edged rocks. She'd been jogging for about a half hour now, and she'd long since passed the point where her lungs ached and her thighs cramped at the exertion. She'd settled into the familiar, easy rhythm of a three-mile-a-day runner and now she could finally clear her mind.

Charlie had introduced her to jogging. He'd been a track star in high school. At sixteen years of age, she would have chased him to the ends of the earth just to attract his attention. She practically did, joining the girls' track team just so they would go to meets together, and have something to talk about. Later, during their married life, they'd done most of their talking while on their morning run.

Jogging was the one thing she'd kept from that earlier life. Over the years she'd grown to love the few moments of solitude. She loved the open air. She loved the way it turned her thoughts away from her troubles, and onto something solid, onto the one thing she could control—the functioning of her own body.

They'd always jogged in perfect rhythm, Charlie and she, which was a product of so many years of shared exercise. She'd been so used to having him by her side that there had been times, after it was all over, when she would be running and her mind was elsewhere, and suddenly she would twist around to say something—to Charlie—only to find, with a jolt, nothing but silence and empty air.

It had been a long time since that had happened. She had been running alone for so long now.

She increased her pace. Streams of golden sunlight filtered down through the leaves, promising a warm bright day for the launch. She *should* be conserving her energy today, not sprinting out into the woods at the crack of dawn. But she'd realized the moment she woke up in Dylan's bed for the second morning in a row that this was her last chance to get away from him—away from his bed, his cabin, his food, his bathroom, his searching gaze—for the next three weeks.

Now *there* was a problem she could focus on. A problem she'd best face right now, if she was to have any peace in the days to come. And face it she would. One hard lesson she had learned in all these years was that she always had to be honest with herself. A person could fool herself into believing a lot of strange things, if she wasn't brutally honest.

The truth was this: It hadn't been so long since Casey had felt a man's admiring gaze. She'd been on a lot of assignments, had met a lot of men. Not all twenty-five-year-old jocks were immune to an older woman's charms. It was just that, in all those years, she had never felt anything in return.

But she lit up like a live wire whenever Dylan was around. She found herself examining the shape of his hands as he held a paddle, the way his hair hung shaggy over his collar. She found herself lying flat on her belly in his bed, naked but for her underwear, spreading her arms across the width of the mattress as if she were making snow angels in the sheets—all the while wondering what the heck she was doing.

Okay, she told herself, taking a deep breath so she wouldn't pass out from lack of oxygen somewhere on this country trail. This shouldn't be a surprise. Jillian had warned her that the time would come when something like this would happen. She even remembered Jillian's words—something about still being a living, breathing woman with a living, breathing woman's needs. At the time, Casey had stared at her as if she'd grown two heads, to think that she could share those kinds of intimacies with any other man but Charlie.

Damn Jillian. In the three years Casey had known her, she'd always been right.

So, Casey thought, feeling the bite of tree bark as she rounded a curve in the narrow path, so she was physically attracted to Dylan MacCabe. She wiped sweat off her brow and smeared it on her gray cotton one-piece jogging suit. Being attracted to a single, handsome, witty, exciting man was a natural enough thing. So she was attracted to Dylan MacCabe. And that was the first step to recovery of any sort—admitting the problem.

So…what was she going to do about it?

She knew that Dylan felt the attraction, too, he'd made that clear enough that first evening. He'd also made it clear that he wasn't looking for anything permanent. Neither was she. But he'd had two wives and who knew how many other women, while the sum total of all her experience was Charlie. She didn't want that experience again. It had taken her too long to pull herself together after he was gone.

She'd long ago made the decision that she would never go back to that old life. She had a new one now: a life of excitement, a life of travel, a life of new experiences every day. She'd chosen it, she'd built it, and she would stick to it.

She closed her eyes and concentrated on the rush of air in and out of her lungs, the throbbing of her heart and the thrum of blood in her ears. She launched herself back down the path, in the direction of the cabin, mulling over the dilemma with each rhythmic step. She was still lost deep in her thoughts as the cabin came into view. She blindly crossed the grass, rounded the Jeep and headed toward the front door.

Then slammed into a man's solid chest.

"Whoa, lady!"

She bounced back in recoil. Two strong hands seized her by the arms, stilling her before she tumbled ungraciously onto her softer side. She struggled to gain a footing, tossed her sweat-drenched hair out of her eyes...and found herself chest-to-chest with Dylan MacCabe.

Dylan, in all his living, breathing glory; Dylan, tousle-haired, stubble-cheeked, looking as if he'd just rolled out of the steamy bedroom of her vivid imagination.

"Dylan..."

His name fell from her lips in a breathless whisper. Even to her ears it sounded seductive. Intimate. Like sleepiness and rumpled sheets.

She felt rather than heard the catch of his breath. His hands tightened on her arms. "Good morning to you, too, Casey."

She licked her lips and tasted the salt of her own sweat. She couldn't help it—she'd just run three miles—she hadn't meant to utter his name like that. Nor had she meant to slam bodily into him. She fixed her gaze on his throat—a safer spot than the darkening blue of his eyes. She noticed her hands lying flat between them, splayed upon his faded tank top as if she were molding his pectoral muscles to her palms.

She yanked her hands away as if they'd been burned. She took two awkward steps back—away from Dylan's rough and ready grin. His gaze fell to her gray one-piece jogging suit, and suddenly the bodysuit felt no more concealing than another layer of skin.

She scraped her palm down the sweat-plastered cloth. "I'm running late."

"You were running, all right," he said gruffly, obviously enjoying the view. "Hard and fast."

She stood, trying to catch her breath, wondering at his tone of voice. "I thought I'd get a few miles in before the launch. I won't be able to run all that much in unfamiliar woods—"

"You shouldn't try so hard, Casey."

She swiped the sweat off her forehead and frowned at him from under her arm. "What do you mean?"

He reached across and traced a trail of sweat down her cheek. "I mean that I'm a pretty nice guy, once you stay still long enough to get to know me."

She froze. His thumb lingered on her jaw while a smile lingered on his lips—a deceptively easy smile. He knew. He knew how she was feeling; he knew why she took such long showers, why she ventured so far out in the woods on her morning runs, why she'd slept in both mornings and gone to bed at the first sign of dusk.

"Why don't you go in and shower." He dropped his hand from her jaw and it was as if he'd stepped back twenty feet. "It'll be your last chance for hot water in three long weeks."

She took him up on his offer and, wordlessly, rounded him to escape through the cabin door.

Within the hour she was steering a wheezing Bessie down the rutted, unpaved road, following Dylan and his laden Jeep into the nearest town. He pulled into a gas station where, the day before, they'd made arrangements to leave her van for repairs. She reluctantly tossed the grizzled mechanic the keys, patted Bessie on the hood, took a deep cleansing breath and climbed into the small cabin of Dylan's Jeep.

He gave her a sexy little smile. "Ready?"

No.

"Yes." She tilted her chin, hated herself for the gesture, then turned away from Dylan so he wouldn't see her misgivings. She caught one last glance of Bessie as they pulled out of the gas station. The mechanic was smoothing an oily rag down the dented hood as he searched for the lever to lift it.

"Are you sure," she asked, "that it's not inconvenient for Daniel to pick up my van?"

"Casey, I told you, he asked to do it," Dylan replied. "Danny feels bad about this whole situation. If it weren't for him, I wouldn't have had to hijack you for this trip."

Hijack you for this trip. She glanced at his profile, wondering if she'd heard a trace of regret in his voice, or if she'd only imagined it. "Did you tell him that the mechanic said it could be days, or even a week, before she's ready?"

"Yeah, yeah, he knows. Danny's staying in his cabin with his wife and kids. 'Recuperating,' is the word he used. He's not going anywhere and he has nothing better to do than wait on Fred's whim."

"But to drive it all the way up to Canada to meet us... Bessie's really temperamental, you know."

"Bessie?"

"My van."

"You named your van?"

"Yeah." She cast him a narrow-eyed look. "You got a problem with that, MacCabe?"

A grin twitched his lips. "Let's put it this way—I haven't named our canoe yet."

"We haven't gone over eighty thousand miles with your canoe, yet."

"Well, I hope you reassured Bessie that she'll be in good hands with Daniel."

She frowned. He made it sound as if she talked to a hunk of metal. She'd hadn't become that lonely in the past three years. "I'm used to her, I know her quirks. Daniel doesn't."

"Hopefully, that mechanic will have gotten rid of those 'quirks' by the time Danny gets his hands on it."

She was acting irrationally. She knew it. But she couldn't get it out of her head that some strange man would be tinkering with Bessie's insides. Tightening her screws. Lubricating her parts. Holding her, driving her, tuning her until she purred and hummed.

For a brief, shimmering moment, Casey wondered who she was thinking about—Bessie or herself.

Dylan turned his Jeep onto the gravel of a launch, just outside of town, then came to a jerking halt. A cluster of well-wishers milled by the riverbank.

"Uh-oh," he muttered.

"What?" She straightened at the sight of his sheepish look. "What is it?"

"The bon-voyage party," he said, gesturing to the fifteen or twenty people now rushing toward the Jeep. "I had hoped they'd forget that today was the launch."

"What's the problem?" she asked, leaning forward. "Are any of them reporters?"

"No. Well, not really." He elbowed his door open with more muscle than was necessary. "But by noon tomorrow all of Bridgewater's going to know that some sleek little brunette took Danny-boy's place."

"What?"

"Brace yourself," he grunted, crunching a heel into the gravel. "You're about to meet the MacCabe clan."

They came at the Jeep like Viking marauders. Tall and blond and red-faced from too much sun. One broad-shouldered bull of a man charged ahead with what sounded suspiciously like a rebel yell. He caught Dylan in the abdomen, then heaved him up with a clank onto the hood of the Jeep. Dylan shoved him off and the two went at it like mountain goats locking horns. The rest of the clan formed a respectable circle around the wrestling pair, and it seemed to Casey that the ones who weren't clucking or shaking their heads were urging the two men on with laughing gusto.

In the midst of the chaos, she swung open the door and stepped out into the sunshine. She moved toward the edge of the circle. A fortyish woman who was definitely a MacCabe turned a streaked-blond head to glance at her, looked back at the wrestlers, then swung her head around to stare at Casey wide-eyed. A well-placed elbow alerted the man beside her, an indelicate grunt alerted the man beside *him,* and within minutes the wrestlers no longer held the attention of the crowd.

The wrestlers noticed the murmuring silence, too, for suddenly they pushed off each other, laughing. The broad-shouldered bull who'd started all the trouble glanced at her, paused, then without hesitation let out a low, long whistle.

"Well, lookee here," he said, shouldering past Dylan. "Dylan's got himself another wife candidate."

Dylan's voice rose amid the rising murmurs. "Bill—"

"The name's Bill MacCabe," the bull said, coming to a halt one step too close to her and flashing a lopsided grin whiter than Dylan's. "And where did my brother find *you?*"

Bill gave her a once-over as thorough as Dylan had given her, and though she didn't experience the same belly-deep frisson, it made her uncomfortable about having chosen to wear a black thigh-length bodysuit.

"The name's Casey," she said, peering over the bull's shoulder toward Dylan's looming form. "And I'd have thought Dylan would have told you I was coming."

"Didn't have a moment," Dylan said, seizing his brother by the scruff of the neck and dragging him back a few feet.

Casey cast Dylan a sidelong look. Didn't have a moment? Didn't they spend the morning in town yesterday, taking care of last-minute details? There were pay phones enough, even in this backwater.

But Dylan ignored her glare and urged her forward with two fingers at the base of her spine. "Folks, this is my new canoeing partner, Casey Michaels."

The questions surged as if in one voice. "What?" "Partner?" "What happened to Danny?" "Where is Danny, anyway?" "Is she joining you and Danny?"

"Danny broke his arm and bruised a couple of ribs on the ski jump last week. Yeah, yeah, he's fine," Dylan added at the feminine gasp. "His pride is bruised more than his ribs. But he's out of the picture as far as the expedition is concerned."

"Lucky you," Bill commented.

"But, Dylan..." The fortyish woman cocked him a look. "You and Danny have been planning this for y—"

"Yeah, and if Danny had thought of that before launching himself headlong off the ski jump, I wouldn't have had to search around for a substitute. As it is, I didn't have to look for one. She came to me." Dylan finally glanced down at Casey. "She's a freelance journalist. She showed up at the cabin looking for a story, and I talked her into joining the expedition with me."

A rumble of suggestive laughter vibrated through the crowd. Casey felt the first heat of embarrassment stain her cheeks. Dylan urged her closer into the circle and began rattling off introductions she knew she would never remember.

Anne, the tall fortyish woman who was apparently Dylan's older sister, curled around the other side of Dylan after the introductions were finished and spoke in a hushed whisper.

"Dylan, are you sure about this? This is terribly last-minute, and such a long voyage—"

"Stop being a clucking hen, Anne. Casey has experience. She's done the Snake River, she can handle this."

Anne pursed her lips and gave Casey the once-over. Casey was beginning to wonder if that manner of seeing through a person with one swift, spearing glance was a family trait. Dylan flattened his hand over the small of her back, as if warning her not to correct him about the Snake River. The truth was, she didn't feel like correcting him, she felt like boxing his ears for putting her on the spot like this.

"Gotta admit, didn't think you had it in you, bro." Bill swaggered back over and smacked Dylan on the chest. "You one-upped me on this one."

Another man wearing wire-rimmed glasses piped up and said, "Isn't there a morals clause in your teaching contract forbidding this kind of behavior?"

"Casey, hon, let's leave the boys to their sports talk," Anne said, disengaging Casey from the flat of Dylan's hand and the brunt of the laughter and innuendo. "I've got a thermos full of hazelnut coffee down here, and I'm sure you're going to need it."

Casey heard Dylan's low laugh as a circle of men closed in around him. "Somehow," she muttered, "I don't think they're talking sports."

"Be sure they're not," Anne said, leading her down the hill to where four boxes of doughnuts and a pile of foam cups teetered on the hood of a car. "Best you get away from that talk or you and Dylan will never patch things up."

"Anne," Casey said, "you're jumping to conclusions—"

"As is everyone else." Anne arched a brow at her. "It's not surprising, you know. Dylan has only brought two women around to meet the family in his whole life, and he ended up marrying them both."

Casey scraped to a stop on the graveled slope.

"Uh-huh," Anne continued, as Casey's jaw grew slack. "That's right. The boy's as faithful as a hound dog—or at least he doesn't brag about his escapades like Bill." Anne rolled her eyes. "I don't think Dylan's ever had an escapade in his life, tell you the truth. He might look like Indiana Jones right now, but you should see him in the classroom—all spit and polish and pressed pants. Want a doughnut?"

Casey shook her head, grappling with an overload of information.

"You should try the Bavarian creams. They're heavenly, and Lord knows, you could use some fat on you."

"Anne, please." Casey rubbed the middle of her forehead. "You've got this all wrong. I'm a journalist. I'm doing this for money."

The pale brows rose high on her forehead, and the blue eyes began to twinkle beneath.

"I didn't mean it like that," Casey corrected, embarrassment mingling with frustration. "I'm on assignment. I'll get paid for the story when it's done."

Anne paused with a sugared doughnut halfway to her mouth. "And then what will you be doing?"

"Leaving," she said. "Following the next story. That's my job."

Anne took a bite, and shook her head as she chewed it down. "Leave it to Dylan. He always picks the same type."

"Excuse me?"

"Oh, it's just that Dylan's a sucker for a certain kind of girl, honey. It's not like the guy isn't ambitious, he's just happy where he is. But he's always picking the kinds of women who'll never settle in Bridgewater."

Casey suppressed the urge to say, *But you don't know me at all. Who says I wouldn't settle in Bridgewater? Or any other fine small town in America?* She'd lived that life once, a long time ago. But she kept her mouth closed. She didn't want to get into that debate. Not here, not now. And not with Dylan's curious sister.

Casey shaded her eyes and gazed up the slope, where the men were still laughing and joking and shoving Dylan and winking, with Dylan in the middle with his smile at full cock and his shoulders in full swagger.

Embarrassment and frustration gave birth to the first frisson of anger.

"Casey," Anne said, "what d'you think about high-school football?"

"Hmm?"

"Football, Casey. Do you watch it?"

"Sometimes. Not for years." Casey shrugged. "I guess I followed it in high school. I was on the track team, and so we followed all sorts of sports."

"Well, that's a plus."

"What?" Casey shook her head. "Why do you ask?"

Anne gave her a mysterious little smile and shrugged a shoulder. "It means there may be hope."

Casey gave her an exasperated look.

"Well, either way, you might as well know right now," Anne said, wiping her sugared fingers on a tiny floral napkin. "I'm absolutely, positively *not* having yet another hideous bridesmaid's dress made. You'll have to settle for one or other of the two—teal with white piping, or burgundy velvet."

Anne's outrageous remark was interrupted by the chatter of the men, as a group of them wove down the slope to the river's edge, hefting the birchbark canoe on their shoulders. Dylan directed the men until the canoe splashed into about two feet of murky water. As they straightened, Casey heard some of the remarks that were not meant for her ears: "Small version of the love boat, if you ask me." "Two one-way tickets to the love lagoon, coming up." "So, did Danny really break his arm or did you toss him out in favor of Legs, there?"

Casey's frisson of anger was stewing into a slow smoldering pique. She stepped away from Anne and waved to Dylan. He gave her a rakish smile and waded through the water toward her. There was an arrogant sway to those shoulders of his, bulging out of the ragged white tank-top he wore, untucked, over a pair of shorts.

As he approached, she wrapped her fingers around the bulge of his forearm. "Let's check the bags, shall we?" she said, mustering a toothy smile. "We have to discuss packing—"

"I'll pack the canoe—"

"Well, I'll supervise. After all, I'll have to know how to do it without the help of your friends and family. And soon." She led him up the slope, through a clutch of men laughing and joking, all the way around to the back of the Jeep. Only then, out of earshot of the harpies, did she drop his arm, swivel one heel in the gravel and face him.

"All right, MacCabe. Are you enjoying yourself?"

He had the nerve to flash her that hundred-watt grin. "Of course I am. I've been waiting for this all year."

"I'm not talking about the launch. I'm talking about this little stunt you pulled."

"Stunt?"

"Playing the dumb jock doesn't flatter you," she said, forcibly lowering her voice so as not to gain the attention of the curious onlookers just by the hood of the Jeep. "Why didn't you tell your family I was coming instead of Danny?"

"I did," he said, dipping his head under the hatchback of the Jeep and searching the mountain of luggage. "I told them just now."

"Yeah, well, why didn't you tell them yesterday? While we were in town in range of a dozen pay phones?"

"I had other things on my mind." He cast her a bright-eyed glance. "Besides," he added, turning back to the wall of gear in search of something, "I knew they'd find out today."

"Oh, they found out, all right." Her gaze drifted toward the hood of the Jeep, where Bill stood with some of the other men, peering at them and grinning. "Is there something wrong with your brother's eyes?"

Dylan seized a handful of duffel bag and yanked, nudging it out of its wedge amid the gear. "What?"

"Bill's eyes," she repeated. "He keeps twitching one at you. Like he has some kind of tick."

Dylan glanced up over the pile of gear and his smile widened at the sight of his brother.

"It must run in the family," she said wryly, "because I just saw you twitch back."

Dylan peered around the edge of the Jeep and hiked the duffel on his shoulder. "Hey, Bill!" he yelled, then heaved the duffel through the air. Bill caught it and skittered back, nearly landing on his rump. "Make yourself useful and take that down to the shore."

Then Dylan turned to her and took a step so they stood

only a hand's breadth away. He cupped her shoulders in his hands.

She supposed he meant to reassure her. She supposed he was trying to treat her like one of his high-school kids grappling with a personal problem. She supposed this was what he usually did in such a situation—take the kid in hand, hold him or her still, and look him or her straight in the eye.

But the moment she felt the scrape of his callused palms on the sun-warmed flesh of her shoulders, her head shot up. A breeze parted the branches of the tree above the Jeep, sending a bright shaft of sunlight against his hair. A surge of blood rushed to her head, making her momentarily dizzy. She met the intensity of that hot blue gaze. And all the anger she felt for him morphed into something far more fierce, far more immediate, far more hungry.

He felt it, too. He opened his mouth but no words emerged. His fingers flexed over her shoulders. His gaze slipped over her face and lingered, a moment too long, on her lips.

"Listen, Casey—" His chest swelled with a deep breath, and he dug his fingers into her skin. "You've got to make allowances for my family. They're loud, they're nosy and they're lacking in social graces—"

"I don't know your family at all," she interrupted. His breath, smelling of strong coffee, brushed her face when he spoke. Her voice sounded husky to her own ears. "I've known them for ten minutes. They've acted perfectly normally, considering the circumstances. It's you I want to pummel."

"Obviously."

"When you told everyone that I was joining you, you were grinning like a cat that had gotten into the cream."

"What did you expect?" He gave her thigh-length black bodysuit a leisurely perusal, and dropped his voice to a whisper. "Have you taken a good look in the mirror lately, Casey Michaels?"

She heard her own sucking intake of breath and hated herself for revealing herself so blatantly. She squeezed her eyes shut for a moment, then shook her head. She couldn't let this happen—she couldn't let him flummox her like this. "The point," Casey persisted, "is that your family believes there is a relationship between us."

"You can't change the way people think."

"Yes, you can. You can tell them the truth."

"Oh, yeah, there's a solution," he said. "Stand up in front of my friends and family and protest loudly that the relationship between us is purely platonic."

"That would have been a good start."

"C'mon. Nobody would have believed us. We'd just be drawing attention to the situation."

"Oh, and showing up with me at the dock without a word of warning wasn't drawing attention to the situation?"

"Casey, I'm thirty-nine. You're of age. What we do as consenting adults is no one else's business."

"That's exactly the problem—you knew damn well what they would think," she said between her teeth, tilting her head with a jerk toward the men clustered at the hood of the car. "Because of you, your family thinks I'm some sort of loose woman, running off with you into the woods for three weeks of skinny-dipping and wild sex."

She could have bitten her tongue off for letting those words leave her lips. Oh, if only the sun could melt her into the ground right now, for Dylan's whole body had tensed and his eyes blazed like all the light of the sky had been harnessed and intensified into some sort of laser beam burning into the part at the top of her head, while she could only stare at the tiny worn hole in his tank top just below

the hem of the neckline, reeling from the images she'd con-
jured up on her own.

Then he loosened his grip on her shoulders, and let his
rough hands slide, slowly, across the muscles and curves of
her upper arms, around her biceps, to palm the points of
her elbows, and run fingers like sparks across the tender insides of her wrists—as a sensualist might run his hands
down the oiled flesh of a naked woman.

Then he asked, in a husky rasp of a voice, "You got something against skinny-dipping?"

Bill stuck his head around the edge of the Jeep. "Skinny-
dipping? Somebody say skinny-dipping?"

They broke apart to the sound of Bill's knowing laughter.
Dylan said something. Casey didn't stay around to hear.
She mumbled some sort of excuse and blindly seized a duf-
fel bag. She tucked it under her arm, turned her back on
Dylan and brushed by Bill to head down the slope, toward
the shore.

Out of the heat of Dylan's touch and into the relative
coolness of the blazing August sun.

DYLAN SPEARED THE TENT stake through two washers and
into the dirt. Curling his hand around the heavy-headed
hammer, he pounded the stake—once, twice—deep into
the ground.

He wished there were twelve stakes instead of six. Hell,
he wished there was no firewood so he could hike away
from this little spit of land he'd chosen for an evening
campsite and cut down an oak. He wished he could find
something to do other than think about what he'd *like* to do
with Casey in this tent, this night.

A whistling rose in the air. He got to his feet and saw
steam spewing from the spout of the kettle on the compact
propane stove. Casey stood still beside it, staring at the

small tent, oblivious to the rising whine of the dented tea-pot.

He'd thought the tent was big enough when he'd envisioned him and Danny-boy drinking beer and cruising these rivers. Now, staring at the lightweight nylon job he'd purchased with some of the grant money, he wished he'd bought a circus tent. Then again, even that wouldn't be big enough to keep him from fantasizing about the feel of Casey under his hands.

He strode to her side, leaned over and shut off the gas for the stove. "We have to ration the propane," he explained, straightening. "The tanks we've got have to last us all the way to Canada."

"Oh."

She tore her gaze away from the tent. She avoided his eyes. She leaned over an open pack filled with freeze-dried meals. Dylan let his gaze skim over her long back, the sun-reddened shoulders, the ridging of her spine pressing against the black bodysuit, the heart-shaped curve of her buttocks.

He swiveled his heel into the dirt and gave one last good shake to the frame of the tent to make sure it was sturdy, though he'd checked it a dozen times already.

She cast a question over her shoulder. "Do you want chicken teriyaki or beef stroganoff for dinner?"

"Beef."

Wordlessly she went about the business of reading the directions and fixing the meal. Their whole day had consisted of such utilitarian conversations. Since the morning with his family, she'd shown, toward him, at least, a brittle coolness that was hiding, he suspected, a simmering anger. From the beginning Dylan had decided to let her stew. He welcomed the distance she forced between them; welcomed it because he was finding it harder and harder to maintain it himself. He shouldn't have touched her as he had behind the Jeep, he should never let this woman come within an arm's length. He had already proved that he couldn't keep his hands off her. He was beginning to wonder how they were going to get through three weeks under such brittle, uncertain conditions.

He strode into the forest to collect wood for a campfire. By the time she'd figured out the simple pour-in-water instructions for the freeze-dried dinners, he'd constructed a worthy blaze to ward off the rising swarm of mosquitos.

He took the aluminum bag steaming with the scent of beef stroganoff and settled down as close to the smoke as he could stand. He started to shovel the food into his mouth. She did the same, perched straight-backed and cross-legged a good distance from him. The fire crackled and popped as it consumed a pine bough woven into the framework of tinder. They ate in silence, watching the flames as the sky turned a darker and darker blue. Soon he'd finished the whole bag of dinner, yet he hadn't tasted one bite of it.

He wadded the aluminum-lined bag into a ball between his palms. They couldn't go on like this for the next three weeks. There had to be some compromise between himself and this woman, something between raucous sex and professional friendship. At the very least, he had to let her know who he was, and what he wasn't.

He was definitely not a man looking for another wife.

"So," he said, as he tossed the ball toward a sack they would use for their garbage. "How long are you going to be angry at me?"

A noodle slipped off her fork and back into her own sack of dinner. She stiffened. "Ah. So you're not a complete dolt."

"It's been the coldest August day I've ever spent."

"I've been waiting for an apology."

"An apology." For what? he wondered. For wanting her? For lusting after her? For thinking about doing what any red-blooded American man would do with a woman on a warm August evening under the stars?

"You should have apologized to me miles ago." Casey waved a fork at him. "That stunt this morning... You set me up, Dylan."

Ah, yes. Now he remembered. That old cow. "No, Casey, I didn't set you up. At least, not intentionally."

"You can't deny you loved every minute of it."

He thought of those few sweaty moments behind his Jeep. "Damn right, I did."

She dropped her fork into her dinner. "There! You don't even deny it!"

"I won't, either." He mustered a grin, though it felt tight against his teeth. "I'm guilty as charged. It's not often I'm in a situation like this."

"Situation like what?"

"Out in the woods," he said, stretching his legs out, "with a good-looking woman."

"Stop it." She said the words swiftly and harshly. Back Off signs were blinking brighter than the flames of the campfire. "Flattery won't get you out of this one, Dylan. Neither will lying."

"I'm not lying."

"You've had two wives and Lord knows how many women before, after and in between, and you're going to tell me you're a thirty-nine-year-old virgin?"

He felt his grin stiffen. He stretched back and wove his hands together, putting them under him as a pillow against the boulder that was his backrest. "Mary-Lou Hetton took care of that when I was—."

"Spare me the dirty details."

"But I may as well be a virgin," he said, trying to keep his voice light, though his grin was fading, along with the images he'd wrestled with on the couch for the past two nights in the cabin. "In this family, Bill's the one who's always caught with his pants down. I'm the staid one. Bill calls me 'Dull-as-Dishwater-Dylan.'"

"C'mon, MacCabe—"

"It's true. That's why the clan couldn't believe it when I showed up with you. And that's why I milked it for all it was worth."

That was the amazing thing about it. Most women didn't pin him for what he was, immediately. Casey looked at him as all the others first looked at him. She didn't see him as the high-school history teacher out on a lark. She knew him only as the adventurer, off for three weeks in the wilderness.

Yeah, and if he looked really hard at it, Dylan knew he'd done all he could to sustain the image. He'd done more wood-chopping in the past few days than he'd ever done. He'd worn all of his working-out-in-the-woods clothes. He hadn't dipped into that old fur-trapper's diary he'd checked out from the local library, nor put on his reading glasses or his chinos, or his leather shoes—all the accoutrements of a history-teacher's uniform. It was hard not to live up to the wrong ideal when a woman as sleek and sexy as Casey Michaels barged into your life.

He was a red-blooded man, after all. And it had been a long time since he'd hankered after a woman the way he hankered after Casey. That was what scared the bejesus out of him.

He'd had two other women who had clung to the same illusion he was presenting to Casey, until the autumn came and the image deteriorated before their very eyes. Until the wedding bands were on their fingers and they'd started liv-

ing the everyday plodding life of the wife of a high-school
teacher. Relationships that started this hot burned out
quickly—and left bitter gray ashes in their wake.

Now here he was, camping in the Adirondack wilderness with a sexy woman, feeling as randy as a teenage boy,
struggling with two equal and opposing forces. He wanted
her, and he wanted to ward her off before the situation got
too hot to handle.

"I think," he began, "that it was the long fishing weekends at the cabin that always clued the ladies in." He stared
up at the canopy of leaves above them, at the last streaks of
blue in the sky. He tried to sound easy and light. "Getting
up at 4:00 a.m. to dig for worms might be a little much for
someone who's used to lingering over the *New York Times*
and coffee until nine."

She said nothing. She remained still. He was glad he'd
chosen this spot to lean back, so he wouldn't have to look
into her eyes.

"Or maybe it was the high-school football games during
the season. It can get really crazy, especially if my team
makes the finals. I admit, the only people who can understand that obsession are adolescent boys and their families.
But there it is.

"Of course, it could have been the family barbecues. You
met the clan—they're enough to drive anyone crazy.
Maybe it was the combination of the three. That's all the excitement Bridgewater has to offer. Pretty dull stuff for most
women."

He heard the creak of the packs rubbing against each
other as she rearranged herself on her makeshift seat. He
bent his knees, easing the pressure on his back.

"So, shoot me," he continued, letting his lips curl back in
a smile that was more grimace than grin. "Let my family
believe whatever they want to believe. Let them think I've

snagged a fine-looking woman for a couple of weeks." He twisted, winked at her, then hiked himself up to poke a stick into the flames. "You've caught me on an upswing, Casey Michaels. Once a year I play Rambo. The rest of the year I'm a boring history teacher who can't keep a wife."

Inwardly he cringed the moment the words left his mouth. He hated making himself look like a pathetic fool. But the words had to be said. She had to know the truth. She had to understand that he would be willing to be her Indiana Jones these weeks, if that was what she wanted; he would be willing to play the part. But she damn well better know that he *wasn't* the part; that he was an ordinary jock from upstate New York who'd had enough heartache to last him a lifetime.

"Lord, the lengths a man will go to rather than say he's sorry," she said, her voice dripping with skepticism. "You're either lying to get my pity, Dylan, or that's the most pathetic attempt I've ever seen of a man trying to be humble."

He blinked at her. The stick he'd been using to stoke the flames caught fire itself. "You don't believe me."

"You're not really blaming your divorces on too many high-school football games and fishing trips?" She dropped her freeze-dried dinner to her side. "C'mon, life is more complicated than that."

"Not around here."

"Then the problem was with the wives, not with the life. Barbecues and fishing trips are what life is made of."

"Listen to you talking," he said, giving the whip-lean brunette with brown lipstick a good once-over. "What the heck would you know about a normal life? With all your gallivanting across the States, chasing one adventure story after another."

She glanced down and her hair slipped across her eyes,

but it left her lips visible, vulnerable in a strange sort of smile. "So you're worried I see you as some sort of Rambo, and here you are seeing me as some sort of globetrotter. Nobody is that simple, Dylan, we're a sum of our parts. And I used to live a 'simple' life like that."

"Get out of here."

"Sure did," she continued. "It wasn't football for me, though. It was track. I was on the team. And we were all quite intense about the meets, I remember that."

He glanced at those long, lean legs splayed out in front of her, and could easily envision her in high-school athletics. "You gave it up after high school, then."

"After college I gave it up. Then I bought an acre of land with a big vegetable garden," she continued. "And a sloppy old mutt I saved from the pound. Called him Poochy."

He couldn't help grinning. "'Poochy?'"

"Yes. Poochy." Her lips twitched into a ghost of a smile that faded more quickly than it was born. "He's living with my sister in Connecticut now. Probably doesn't remember me at all."

"What happened?"

He'd asked too bluntly. She glanced at him, and it was as if she'd been shaken from a trance. Her amber gaze slid away as quickly as it had come. Along with the fragile thread of easy goodwill that had just begun to stretch between them.

"Well...I had to give it up." She pursed her lips, then shook her head, once. "No. I *chose* to give it up. To chase other dreams."

Her words hit him like a blow to the head. She chose to give up a simple life. To chase other dreams. Like his first wife. Like his second wife.

"If you don't mind, Dylan," she said, getting to her feet,

oblivious to the havoc she'd just wreaked upon him, "I think I'm going to call it a night. I'm exhausted, and these mosquitos don't seem to mind the repellent."

"Take the propane lamp," he muttered, gesturing to the lamp on top of a pile of their gear. "I'll be in...in a while."

He turned back to the flames, away from her. He listened to her rustle among the packs. He heard the clank of the handle of the propane lamp, the zip of the nylon tent flap, the rustle of her feet upon the nylon flooring. He imagined her stretching to get out of the oversize sweatshirt she'd donned when the sun set. He imagined what she would look like, peeling off her clothes, one layer at a time.

He wondered what kind of underwear she wore. Whether she was a cotton-panties type of woman, or whether she opted for silky slips of things edged in lace and cut high so those long, lean legs looked even longer.

Almost against his will, he found himself swiveling in the dirt to glance at the tent, which was lit from within by the golden glow of the propane lamp.

He watched the shadow of that woman he could not have, as she pulled the sweatshirt over her head. Her hair swung against her shoulders, and he could see her body, outlined starkly against the nylon tent.

He knew he should turn away. He told himself to turn away as she slipped one shoulder out of her bodysuit, then the other. But as she began to peel the whole thing down over her ribs and past the sucked-indentation of her belly, he knew he couldn't turn away even if a bear had come rumbling up behind him.

The light cast her form in sharp relief, showing the swell of her breast, even the nub of her nipple, uptilted and sweet—then hidden behind the shadow of her arm as she shifted to slip the bodysuit down under her bottom and across those legs—now sharp again, silhouetted against the pale glow of the tent....

Then, somehow, he was there—just outside the tent—reaching out to trace, ever so gently, the rise and curve of that shadow of a breast, wishing he were touching warm puckered flesh and not cold nylon fibers. Wishing he had that hard nub against his tongue, suckling, while she made noises in her throat.

What kind of noises would she make? Would she talk while she made love, would she guide him with her hands, or would she hold him hard while she struggled with the same intensity of passion that now flowed through him...?

He shoved his hands into his pockets to ease the pressure of his shorts against his loins. He couldn't go into that tent. Not now. Not in an hour. Not until long after he heard the soft, deep sound of her breathing. He wondered how bad the mosquitos would be if he laid his sleeping bag by the fire. He wondered if he would ever get to sleep.

He lifted his face to the heavens and stared at the blur of stars. And he told himself, over and over, that he would be damned if he would make the same mistake thrice.

6

"LET'S TAKE A BREAK." Dylan held his paddle a hairsbreadth above the water and scanned the rocky shore. "There," he said, pointing to an outcropping. "A good place for a swim."

Casey glared at his broad, tanned back. They'd been paddling since first light and her arms felt like overcooked linguine. "A swim, MacCabe? Or laps?"

He twisted with a stroke and flashed her a wicked grin. "A little touchy this morning?"

"Just wondering if this is a canoe trip or training for the triathlon. You must make one heck of a football coach."

"The boys don't complain."

"I suspect the boys don't *dare* complain. You'd probably assign them push-ups or chin-ups or some other indescribable torture."

He laughed easily. The sound rang out over the clear water. "This swim will be for pure pleasure. This will be the last open water we'll see for a while."

Casey burrowed deeper into her black mood. Sure, *he* could laugh. The sun of the past two days had done no more than burnish his tan. Her shoulders itched and peeled from her foolishness yesterday, when she'd forgotten to reapply sunscreen in the afternoon. He could cover up his unwashed hair with a baseball cap. She had to be satisfied with sweeping her lifeless hair up in barrettes and pins that left tickling strands dripping across her face. He looked rakish with bristle on his face. Her legs, on the other hand, were looking just plain hairy.

She had forgotten why she disliked camping so much. Sunscreen and mosquito repellent pooled oily on her throat, under her breasts, between her toes. Splashing her face with lake water every morning just couldn't take the place of a piping-hot shower—but it would be two weeks and four days before she felt that again.

All in all, she was feeling jumpy and wretched and completely out of sorts. She needed a shower. She needed a fresh salad. She needed some breathing room.

She helped pull the canoe up on a little spit of shore, curled deep within a sheltered cove. He leaped out with all the grace of a cat. She splattered into the cool water. She grimaced as she helped beach the canoe and secure it. She couldn't help it. Her arms ached from the exertion, and her neck was stiff from sleeping on the hard ground on the wrong side. Her left side. She was used to sleeping on her right side, but in the tent they shared, Dylan slept against the left wall.

At least, she thought he did. She'd never actually *seen* him sleep, although she discovered, every morning, his rumpled sleeping bag lying beside hers. He claimed he came in after she'd already fallen asleep, and woke up long before she rose. With the way she'd been tossing and turning every night, anxious for his arrival, that meant he was subsisting on a fraction of the amount of sleep she was getting, which wasn't much at all.

She turned away abruptly from the object of her thoughts, yanked off her T-shirt, snapped the barrette holding her hair up, and with a running jump, dived right into the water.

The water sluiced over her like cool gentle hands, and by the time she surfaced in the sunshine by the edge of the cove she felt a layer of mosquito repellent and sunscreen peel away. It would be nice to have a big, blowup float. It would be nice to have someone swim a strong icy Piña Colada out to her waiting hands.

She heard Dylan's splash and turned in time to see him surface, a few feet away.

Grinning. All white teeth in a tanned face. All bright, twinkling eyes. All grizzled and wet and wickedly naked from the waist up.

"So," she said, sinking her water shoes into the soft bottom, "what did you mean when you said this was the last open water for a while?"

"We're moving from ponds to creeks soon. Shallow and meandering little rivers. Shouldn't see another pond until we're practically in Canada." His gaze flickered down her body, and she wondered if wearing her bright pink bikini had been the wisest thing to do this morning. "You'll get a rest from paddling, but we'll be portaging more."

"Great. From Olympic rowing to world-class weight lifting." She raked her fingers in her hair, vigorously scratching her itchy scalp. "Now you're really going to wish Danny-boy was here."

"Dan would be complaining about the mosquitos. And the lack of beer. And moaning that he had no time to fish." He fell back in the water and lay, floating. He added, with a twinkle, "You're doing all right, Casey. That is, for a girl."

One well-aimed splash left him sputtering in his mirth. She waded past him toward the stern end of the canoe. She rifled around until she found her personal bag, tucked securely between two rucksacks, then tugged out a small white bottle.

She looked him square in the eye as she waded deeper, waving the shampoo. "It's biodegradable."

He swiped his face with his forearm. "Yeah?"

"It's made from the yucca plant. I made sure of it before I bought it. So I'm not burying the suds, do you hear?"

His Viking gaze fell upon the bottle suspiciously.

She halted, hiking a hand on her hip. "I'm not packing them in, either, MacCabe."

"You know the rules, Casey." A wicked gleam lit his eye. "Take only pictures, leave only footprints."

"And look like a grizzly bear by the time you get back to civilization."

"You don't look anything like a grizzly bear."

She blinked up at him. The sunlight shone through the leaves above, dappling spotted light upon the water. Dylan suddenly seemed bigger. Taller. Stronger. She had an eerie sense of isolation, as they both stood here in the water of an unnamed lake, far from civilization. It had been over twenty-four hours since they'd even seen a stray hiker.

She felt light-headed, as if she'd stood up too abruptly.

Dylan jerked his chin toward the bottle. "Will that stuff put you in a better mood?"

"Huh?"

"The shampoo," he said, gesturing to the bottle still gripped in her hand. "Washing your hair. Will it wipe that scowl off your face?"

Lately, she didn't know what would put her in a better mood. Sleep might. Or a morning without the shock of stumbling out of the tent to find him, tanned and wet and *male*, waiting for her with a coffee cup in his hand.

The thought brought fresh heat to her cheeks.

"It'll help," she said, snapping open the bottle. "At this point, any creature comfort would help."

"Then let me."

He slipped the bottle out of her hand. Before she could react, he'd poured a glob into his palm, tucked the bottle inside the waistband of his swimsuit, and laid his hands upon her head.

She might have gasped aloud. She thought she had. She might have tried to jerk away. She thought she had. But at the first touch of his hands a rush of sensation blinded her, and she stood stiff in the midst of the wave, taking the onslaught until it ebbed away—leaving her tingling with shock and conscious only of the here and now.

The shine of the wet whorls of hair upon his chest. The smell of a man's sun-warmed skin, of heated aloe. The screech of a blue jay, high up in the trees. The slap of the cool water against her midriff, against his abdomen. The light pressure of his fingers on her scalp.

He worked the shampoo through her hair. He had big, strong hands. He knew what he was doing. He knew how to touch, he knew where to press. He worked the foam all over her head, but his fingers did more than shampoo her hair. He pressed his thumbs against her temples, kneaded the part in her hair with his knuckles. He massaged the top of her head with the pads of his fingertips, then worked his way to the base of her neck and kneaded every taut, knotted muscle.

She made a sound. Almost a moan. She heard herself as if from far away, for the tension of the past week melted under his fingers, and all of a sudden she wished that she could dissolve into the water and sleep. She wished, too, that he would go on massaging her scalp like this forever. She wished he would do her shoulders...her arms...that ache in the hollow of her back.

She didn't know how long she stood, her head wobbling as he massaged her, finding the hollows behind her ears, massaging her hairline, digging his thumbs into the ridge at the nape of her neck. Until, suddenly, he took his hands away.

She swayed as she blinked her eyes open.

"Rinse," he said in a ragged voice.

She responded by instinct. She dipped back into the water, submerged herself, and ran her fingers through her suddenly soft hair. A cloud of foam surrounded her, then swiftly dispersed. She propelled herself, face first, out of the water, raking her hair away from her forehead.

Then, suddenly, Dylan's warm lips slid against her skin.

She knew they were his lips, though her eyes were still closed from the sting of the soapy lake water. She knew the roughness of that bristled cheek against her temple, she knew the smell of him from the long nights in the tent that seemed as small as a closet. She knew the feel of his lips against hers, remembered from that brief kiss they'd shared, the very first day they met.

It seemed she'd been waiting every moment since, for the taste of that mouth again.

She turned her face to meet his lips. She hadn't consciously meant to do that, she told herself, anticipating the touch of his mouth upon hers; she really hadn't meant to do this at all.

Their lips met, and merged in a breath. Loosened, then merged again. There was a pause—uncertain and tense—their lips apart only by moisture, only by a breath. Then another merging, another kiss; deeper this time, more intent.

He knew how to kiss. He knew how to suckle her upper lip into his mouth, then suckle the bottom one, too; he knew how to make her open her mouth and invite him deeper. He knew how to make her keep kissing. He knew how to make her forget herself.

For this wasn't her, standing waist-deep in lake water with the shadows of the trees shivering over them.... This wasn't her, arching her neck and offering her mouth to Dylan MacCabe, leaning ever so slightly forward, into him, so that her wet breasts brushed his damp chest. No, no, this wasn't Casey Michaels. She didn't know this woman standing in her place, losing herself in the quiver of Dylan's kiss. This woman was uninhibited, this woman felt sexy and sure and full of yearning. This woman was *giving* herself to him, without a second thought.

Then, suddenly, Dylan lifted his head. And Casey stood swaying, blinking up at him. Her lips throbbed, felt puffy and swollen.

He scanned her face with those intense blue eyes. Searching for something. She noticed a small scar that cut across the bristle on the tip of his chin. Gold tipped each of his lashes.

The shock ebbed away. She'd just kissed Dylan Mac-Cabe. Freely. Willingly. And with feeling.

He let his hand slide out of her hair.

"I'm not saying I'm sorry, Casey."

She stared at him. Words wouldn't form in her throat. She didn't know what to say, anyway. All she knew was that with one kiss, Dylan had turned her into a woman she didn't know. A responsive woman. A vulnerable woman. Dylan had made her want something she'd convinced herself she would never have again.

"I've wanted to do that since the first time I kissed you in the cabin." His hands lay still at his sides, but he stood as coiled and tense as a spring. "I'm going to do it again, Casey, and this time I'm not stopping—"

"No."

She stumbled back in the water, away from him, sending up a surge of spray. She stilled just as swiftly as she'd moved, surprised at her own reaction.

She looked away from him, away from those fierce confused eyes. She needed to figure out what was going on in her head that had allowed her to fall so easily into Dylan's arms. She needed time to think. She needed to get away from him.

All around her was the lapping silence of the northern woods, and the knowledge that she *couldn't* get away from him—not for weeks.

Panic gripped her. Turning away from Dylan's strong, sure presence, she took a deep breath—a deep, cleansing breath—and tried to get a hold of herself.

She heard him breathing. She heard him waiting. Her tongue felt heavy and unresponsive in her mouth. "That wasn't on the agenda, MacCabe."

"Yeah, well, that's the thing about travel," he said, his voice filled with frustration. "It's full of surprises."

"Keep your surprises to yourself. And let's keep this all business."

She heard the water, felt the ripples of his movement, and jerked away before he could touch her.

"Casey, we could light up most of Bridgewater with the electricity between us." He lowered his voice. "You feel it, too."

She bristled. He'd breached her defenses, and it made her angry that he would use that knowledge against her. "I didn't come out here looking for a lover."

"Neither did I." The water gurgled as he shuffled where he stood. "I didn't plan this. But now it's happened."

"Nothing has happened," she retorted, hating the hoarseness of her voice. "Nothing of significance."

"Oh, yeah? Then why won't you look at me?"

She looked at him. She didn't want to. But she twisted abruptly and looked straight into those intense blue eyes with Jillian's words ringing in her ears:*"Face what you fear, Casey. It's the only way you'll conquer it."* A shiver shuddered through her as she met Dylan's bright eyes, a quiver that shook her right down to her toes. A tremor that had nothing to do with cold or fear or dread—and everything to do with passion.

She didn't want this. She'd never wanted it. Yet standing here before him, she had a fierce sense of inevitability.

She remembered the dress she'd worn that first night, that little slip of silk. And the bright pink bikini she'd chosen to wear this morning. And the way she'd stretched yesterday as she'd risen from brushing her teeth, knowing Dylan's eyes were upon her. She remembered, too, the discreet little purchase she'd made at the drugstore the day before the launch.

She'd willed this upon herself. Not consciously, no. But she couldn't stand here and deny that she'd wanted to kiss him from that very first day. And more. Her body did, at least. Her body still craved much, much more. She'd been too cowardly to admit it to herself.

She'd forgotten what it was like to be so close to another human being; she'd forgotten the joy of flesh upon flesh, of lips upon lips. She'd forgotten what it felt like to have blood rushing through her veins—not from running a track, but from doing something no more physical than rubbing cheeks with a man.

She knew then that, sooner or later, she was going to become Dylan MacCabe's lover.

The thought shocked her to the bone. She couldn't. She couldn't make herself that vulnerable again. Not here, not yet, not now—not ever.

"Look, Dylan," she said, speaking as calmly as she could—more to herself than to him. "We hardly know each other. Yet we've spent every moment together for a week."

"Is that what it is, Casey? Just the moment?"

"Yes," she said emphatically. "You're single, I'm single, the sun is bright, the water warm. Let's just write this whole thing off to the situation and move on, okay?"

A muscle flexed in his cheek. He looked at her—a long, long look that held her when she would have glanced away.

"That ain't going to be easy, Casey. Not anymore."

"ARE YOU EVER GOING to give me my own copy of that map, or are you going to pore over it all by yourself for the whole trip?"

Dylan eyed Casey sitting pertly at the stern, then swiftly drew his attention back to the laminated map he'd balanced on one knee. He didn't need another look at her to know her hair had dried soft and shiny in the breeze, a result of that intense shampooing session they'd shared in the cove.

"There are two streams that lead into this part of the lake," he said, trying to keep his voice conversational. "I'm trying to figure out which of the two is the right one to take."

"If I had my own map, I could help."

"Can you say 'Eeny, meeny, miney, mo'?"

"Just as well as you, I suppose."

"Here, then. This will be yours." He snapped the map back to her, and avoided her arched eyebrow. He dug another copy out of the waterproof map cylinder snug under his seat. "I've marked where we are. You see we're entering the streams now. The map only indicates one outlet at this end of the lake, but we've found two."

"What's this strange mark a couple of miles up the stream?"

"A marker. A rock carving. Probably petroglyphs."

"Petroglyphs? You mean...prehistoric carvings of some sort?"

"Indian carvings, more likely. But yeah, that's right."

"But you told me this map was written three hundred years ago."

"Yeah?"

"But any rock carvings that existed then could be faded. Covered by bushes, by trees, or just worn away. How are we to be sure the rock carvings are still there?"

"We aren't." He grinned back at her, though his heart held no humor. "That's the beauty of this trip, Casey. It's full of surprises."

He was rewarded with the sight of her flush. He turned away swiftly. He had to stop staring. He'd stared enough in the past few days to imprint the sight of her on his mind as surely as petroglyphs in the granite rock of the Adirondacks. He couldn't seem to stop looking at her, even if it was as simple as watching her bend over a river as she brushed her teeth. He'd found infinite fascination in the way her hair slipped over her shoulders...in the curve of her lean back...

She was driving him crazy. He was a grown man, but she had him feeling like a randy teenager. His nights were filled with fantasies of rolling that few feet of distance between them, and peeling that slim-fitting tank top she always wore to bed right off her body, so he could see without impediment the peaks of her breasts, see whether her nipples were pale and tender and pink, or as luminescent as her eyes. Then, covering one with his mouth to taste her—

Stop! She was skinny, he told himself. He could see the ribbing of her spine whenever she bent over. She was small-breasted, lean-hipped. He liked his women with curves and heft—more to grab on to, no fear of bruising anything in the heat of the moment.

The moments were getting hot enough around here.

He'd been spending far too much time thinking about

her, and him, and *it*. He should be concentrating on the map balanced on his knee, or the choices spread out before him—the wide inlet on his right, and the smaller inlet farther down the banks on his left—both equally viable alternatives. He should be thinking about the journey, concentrating on all he remembered of what his aging grandfather had said about this trip in his more lucid moments. He shouldn't be thinking about the feel of Casey's shampoo-slick hair in his palms, or the brush of her breasts against his chest.

"Seems to me," she said, as she absently stroked the paddle to keep the canoe still, "that the petroglyph — or whatever it is — should be two to six miles or so upstream, right?"

He snapped the laminate flat, though he knew the map by heart. "I calculate four miles."

"Well, let's pick a path and go looking for it."

"If we're wrong, it means backtracking. Double the mileage, half the time."

"Well, from what I can see, there's no way of knowing which is the right way by this map."

"That's right."

"Then I say 'Eeny, meeny, miney, mo.' Right fork."

Dylan shoved the map between his feet. "Right fork it is."

He dug his paddle deep, shoved it hard, then lifted his face to the breeze. He directed the nose of the canoe up the wide inlet, into the unknown.

He tried to sweat away the thoughts. He paddled strenuously. In the river, the current flowed against them. Not too strong, not yet, though he imagined the narrower the stream became, the more swift the current, and the harder they would have to work to travel any distance. True to form, as the stream suddenly constricted, the current seized the belly of the canoe. He paddled deeper. He sensed her struggling to keep pace, but he didn't stop. He wanted his muscles to hurt tonight. He wanted to go to bed in that tent and *sleep*. He wanted to concentrate on pain, instead of pleasure denied.

Not for the first time, he wondered what the story was between her and her husband. He wondered what the hell the bastard had done to make her so reticent, to make her so closed, so distant; so fiercely determined to resist the rush of electricity humming between them.

The attraction was mutual. That much he knew, now. For a moment back at the cove, she'd been yielding and open, and the current had flowed strong through them both.

He hadn't wanted this to happen. He wasn't looking for a woman—he'd had two too many—and least of all, for a woman who would, at the end of this journey, climb back in her van in search of another assignment. Leaving him here picking up the pieces while the members of the clan MacCabe shook their heads and muttered among themselves, "At least he didn't marry this one, before she dumped him."

But he was a man, after all. And she was all woman. And the weather was hot and humid and the water was cool and clear. He didn't know how much longer he could play the gentleman, while the bees buzzed in his ears and the birds chirped in the trees.

"Dylan?"

He tightened his grip on his paddle. Her voice was soft, and it grazed against his senses. "You want a break?" he asked.

"No...but isn't it getting dark?"

He blinked at the world around him. The pines rose straight on either side of the river, and only a funnel of sky peeked between the dark green tips. He'd been so lost in his thoughts, he hadn't noticed the change in the weather. The wet wind winnowed through the trees. The black bellies of clouds billowed in the sky above.

He muttered, "A storm's coming."

Fast and furious, judging by the roiling of the sky. He glanced around, but there was no place to land. Underbrush billowed from the steep banks and dipped the tips of greenery in the water. He caught sight of a mallard in the shelter formed by the brush, already hiding from the coming rain.

He added, "We've got to find a place to pitch the tent."

She must have heard an urgency in his voice, for she paddled with renewed strength. They rounded a curve in the river and he caught sight of a small spit of rocky shore just as the first thick raindrops splattered the surface of the water.

By the time they'd pitched the tent on the uneven ground and covered the canoe with a tarp, rainwater had soaked them to the skin. He stumbled into the tent with the last of the supplies and swiped the water out of his eyes. Casey sat on the nylon floor, rubbing a towel briskly through her hair.

At the sound of supplies dropping, she peeked out from under the towel. Rainwater pattered on the tarp above his head. The coolness of a puddle gathered around his feet.

Casey's body steamed from exertion. Her T-shirt clung to her body, revealing every line of the hot-pink bikini, shaped the curve of her thigh, draped off the line of her shoulder. The tent smelled of her—and of the faint floral fragrance of the shampoo they'd shared that afternoon.

He realized that it couldn't be five o'clock yet—hours and hours before he would have the urge to sleep.

He turned his back to her and unzipped one of the packs. He rifled around for his own towel, then wrestled off his

T-shirt. He used his towel as a screen as he shimmied off his bathing suit.

He heard, behind him, a rustle of clothing, and realized she, too, was peeling off her wet clothes.

It would be so easy. Just to turn around. To see the curve of that back uninterrupted by the strap of a bathing suit. To see the tight mounds of her bottom, no longer hugged by cotton. To see the perkiness of her breasts, free of the tautness of a bathing suit, unobscured by the white cotton of an old T-shirt. His palms itched to feel her naked flesh, or her clean sleek hair....

He closed his eyes, thinking, *Death, gloom, pestilence.* Anything to soften the decided rise of the towel draped around his waist. This afternoon she'd made it as clear as glass that she didn't want his kiss, his touch, or his lovemaking. *Famine. War. Losing in the fourth quarter on a third down.* He struggled into a pair of loose, dry shorts though his legs still dripped with water.

When he was sure she'd settled down, he glanced at her over his shoulder. She wore an oversize T-shirt with the logo of a famous rock band. She was sucking on an end of her hair. She looked about sixteen.

Yeah, that's it, MacCabe. She's too young for you.

Of course, he felt about twenty right now. With just about as much control over his body.

She glanced at him from over the edge of a paperback she'd been reading since the first day. Obviously, she wasn't making much progress.

She let the book drop to her lap. "Know any good ghost stories, Dylan?"

He met those big, amber eyes, and saw in them a mutual acknowledgement that it was going to be a long and difficult night. Saw more, too; more than he wanted to see. A vulnerability. A silent plea.

"Nope," he said, in a voice that was more growl than anything. "Haven't done the Boy Scout thing in years."

He plunked down and rifled through the packs piled between them, looking for something to eat that wasn't a granola bar, peanut butter and crackers, or dried apricots. A beer would be nice. Or a bone to nosh on, to grind out his frustrations.

He suddenly had a new take on the expression "cabin fever."

Jolting herself upright, she said, "I have an idea."

She leaned over the packs. Her T-shirt gaped. His gaze fell to the line of her throat, and lower, to the white curve of a breast.

He cracked his elbow on a rock jutting under the nylon as he forced himself back down. He sank his teeth into a hunk of salami and worked his jaw to chew it.

"I've got it." She settled back, cross-legged, and gave him a tentative smile. "I assume you play cards, MacCabe."

"Wednesday nights," he said, talking around the salami. "My night out with the boys."

"Good." She snapped out the cards and nimbly shuffled them. "So, what'll it be? Gin rummy? Five-card stud, joker's wild?"

He tore off another hunk of salami. "How 'bout strip poker?"

He couldn't bite back the words. He didn't want to. After this afternoon, he couldn't pretend that he didn't want to flatten her against the floor of the tent and let nature take its wild and heated course.

The cards shuffled to a stop in her palm. She narrowed a look at him, frowning. "High hopes, huh?"

He shrugged. "A man's got to try."

"Well, why don't we start with something a little less...risky. Like 'Go fish.'"

He grunted and stared at the red backs of the cards she dealt his way.

It was going to be a hell of a long night.

7

CASEY STEPPED OUT OF the canoe and splashed into the shallows. She sank ankle-deep into the silty riverbed.

"Great. Just great," she groaned. She lunged toward the bank. Her heel slipped against a rock and sank deeper. She sucked her back foot out of the mud. The fine silt seeped in under the edges of her sagging socks. By the time she splashed to the dry riverbank her legs were black from the mid-calf down and grit seeped between her toes.

Dylan, tying the towrope to a branch overhanging the bank, cast her a vaguely amused glance. "Missed the rocks, eh?"

"No, Dylan," she snarled. "I actually wanted to be exfoliated from the knees down."

"That works better with your sneakers off."

"No kidding."

She cast him a black look. His boots were squeaky-clean. Of course he didn't sink into the mud. Of course not. Mr. Sensible Nature Man probably mapped out the route before he stepped out of the canoe.

"Just think of it this way," he said, tightening the rope with practiced ease. "The mud's good for mosquito bites."

She glared at him as she scratched her arm, where a series of welts glowed red along her elbow. She felt her cheeks flush with irritation and anger. She had a sudden image in her head of Wile E. Coyote, eyes red in fury, steam belching from his ears. She only wished she had the phone number for the Acme Company.

Mr. Optimist was beginning to get on her nerves.

Of course, everything was beginning to get on her nerves. First of all, the rain. Not drenching downpours of rain, no. Not enough to convince Mr. Nature Boy to put up the tent and take cover for a while, but spitting mist, instead. A spitting mist that made her normally straight, sleek hair kink and twist like Little Orphan Annie's. A vague drizzle that seeped under the collar of her T-shirt and made her as itchy as if she had an all-body case of diaper rash.

For two days this haze had fallen on them. Two days of pewter skies and fog. Two nights of sleeping wet without a fire. Two days of living under this Saran Wrap rain poncho feeling like some kind of soggy leftover.

Two days of wondering what had possessed her to agree to take this trip with this infuriating go-go football coach, this disgustingly well-conditioned hunk who could still look heart-stoppingly good, unshaven and soaking wet, after a week of roaming the woods.

"I'm going to climb that rock," he announced, checking the rope for tautness and eyeing the float of the canoe. "Maybe I can find that Owl's Head landmark better from up there."

"According to your inaccurate ancient map," she said, kicking her muddied foot against a sapling, "we were supposed to be able to see Owl's Head Rock from the river."

"Yeah, yeah, but maybe the trees have grown. Maybe there's a petroglyph we can't see from below. Maybe the rock formation has eroded. We're not getting anywhere looking from the river, so we might as well scout out the terrain."

"Yes, sir, Mr. Eagle Scout." She mocked a salute as she

scraped her other muddy shoe against the sapling. They'd spent the whole morning looking for "Owl's Head Rock," a supposedly prominent landmark on the route, to no avail. "So," she said, "we're lost."

"Casey, don't start this again." His jaw set. "We're not lost."

"No?"

"*No.*"

He swept up his pack and hefted it over those brawny shoulders, then swung a rope over one arm. *We'd better not be lost,* she thought darkly. He might think he was Indiana Jones, but Casey knew she was not—nor would she ever be. Beef jerky and freeze-dried chicken teriyaki was one thing, but she wasn't going to live on wild onion grass and well-baked acorns and various other disgusting survival foods while he sent smoke signals for help, just because this adventurer felt like playing Davy Crockett. She had her own plans for rescue tucked tight in her backpack, if they did ever find themselves truly lost in the wilderness.

"You're not one of those guys who refuses directions, I hope," she said, slapping her hands free of muck. "The kind that will drive in circles with a map on the steering wheel muttering to themselves, instead of admitting that just maybe, just *maybe*—"

"Six hours ago we entered this stream. The turnoff is clear on the map."

"Ah, yes, old Henri's trusty three-hundred-year-old map—"

"If worse came to worst," he interrupted, "we could backtrack to that point."

"I say, that means we're lost."

"No. We're not lost."

She stilled. So she'd finally probed a sore spot in the optimist's armor. His jaw was set, his shoulders stiff. A muscle flexed in that ill-shaven cheek.

Then he looked up and his bright blue gaze swept over her, from dripping hair to dirty toes. "You can stay here while I climb," he said. "Throw up a tarp. I'll be back within the hour."

He turned on his heel and crashed, alone, into the woods.

Casey stood in the dim gray light for a moment, staring at the greenery swaying in the wake of his departure, staring at the darkness of the woods beyond, listening to the crackling of litter, the creaking of tree branches bowing under the weight of rain. She thought of the bull moose they'd passed yesterday, its huge antlers dipping as the animal drank at the riverbank. Then, with one swift move she swung up her own discarded pack.

"Wait!" She crashed through the woods, pushed away ferns and branches, and caught up with him. "Wait, Dylan—"

He came to an abrupt halt as he swung to face her. "What is it?"

Whip-crack sharp. Impatient. His eyes a bright blue in the dimness. And all of a sudden the air was full of lightning.

She took a step back. Damn him. Damn him for looking so good while she felt like a limp noodle. Damn him for *looking* at her...like that.

Didn't he think she was angry, too? Didn't he know she sensed the frustration shimmering between them? Didn't he know she tossed and turned in her sleeping bag every night, all her senses directed toward him lying on the other side of the tent, as if her body consisted of a hundred thousand magnetic needles, all straining north? She wanted to be rid of him, too, but they were stuck here together and that was what was causing all this friction.

She forced herself to meet his eyes. "I'm coming with you, Dylan."

"Why?"

"Why not?"

"Because you don't have to prove anything to me."

He straightened. His chest expanded as he took a deep breath. She tore her gaze from the way the damp cotton of his T-shirt clung to his pectorals. He looked beyond her, over her shoulder, away from her face. She saw his struggle in the tightness of his features.

"Listen," he said finally, in a voice falsely calm, "you've been a real trooper, but I can do this better alone."

She narrowed her eyes. He did that often lately. Called her a "real trooper." Or urged her to paddle yet another mile, saying, "Come on, girl, you can do it." He did everything but pat her on the head when she managed a difficult task. She wondered if he would offer her a Girl Scout badge when this was all over.

She supposed it made him comfortable that way—to put them in the role of teacher and student. Instead of what they really were. Instead of what they could not avoid facing, each evening, stuck inside that small tent in the dark, or even now, in the moist intimacy of these woods. They were just one man and one woman, out in the wilds. Alone. With lightning arcing between them.

"No way, MacCabe," she said, wondering at the quiver in her voice. "I'm not waiting back there alone."

"There's nothing to be afraid of in these woods."

"No, nothing but a bull moose in rut and a bobcat or two—"

"Casey, there are no—"

"Besides," she interrupted, in no mood for logic, "you need me."

The muscle in his cheek flickered again. A light in his

eyes flared. She realized there was more than one truth in those words.

He curled his hand over the binoculars hanging from his neck. "I can use these well enough myself."

"You need my perspective," she persisted. "That's what partnership is all about, right?"

His knuckles whitened on the binoculars. Then, with a grunt, he swiveled a foot in the muck. "Suit yourself, then."

As soon as he turned away her breath rushed out of her in one long swoosh. She closed her eyes, then shook herself out of light-headedness. He'd already surged too far ahead, and she was determined not to be left behind.

She caught up to him and followed his long-legged stride as best she could. He was making no allowances for her now. Not that he ever had, since that afternoon in the cove. He seemed to take great pleasure in pushing her—and himself—to the edge of endurance. She felt as if she'd spent the last week trying to catch her breath.

She plodded on. Her feet squelched in river silt and water with every step. She was so wet. From the inside of her ears to the inside of her toes. From the back of her neck to the base of her spine. She couldn't help but think of hot baths and heated rooms, she couldn't help but crave civilization. She wanted to find a Laundromat, hurl herself bodily into one of those industrial three-load dryers, close the door and let the thing whirl her until she tumbled out, as dry and soft and fluffy as a big terry-cloth towel.

She also wanted a good meal. A *cooked* meal. Something that wasn't powdered or freeze-dried. She wanted a big glass of orange juice. She wanted dry socks. She wanted to sleep on a mattress. She wanted to sleep with Dylan.

She wanted to sleep with Dylan.

She jerked her backpack tight against her shoulders. Dylan had done it to her again. Thoughts like that always struck her when she was in extremes of physical exertion. Like now. Like at the end of a five-mile jog. It had always been during those mini-marathons that she had seen through her problems most clearly. That was the real problem here, if she admitted it to herself. She wanted to sleep with Dylan MacCabe.

Suddenly, Jillian's voice rang in her head—so clearly that Casey imagined she could even smell Jillian's cigarette smoke.

There will come a time, Casey, when you'll want a man in your bed again. It's a normal biological response.

Casey tightened her grip on her backpack and wondered how Jillian managed to do that—plant some key phrases in her head and then send her off so that whenever Casey hit an emotionally fragile situation those phrases would sound in her head, like an audiotape on a loop.

She raised her glance to Dylan. He strode purposefully ahead of her. The mist had soaked his shirt and made it cling to his shoulder blades—to the width of those shoulders, to the hollow at the base of his back just above his belt. Something fluttered deep inside her, something that made her knees go weak.

Oh, God, I'm not ready for this.

She squeezed her eyes shut. She wasn't ready for any of it. The idea. The *wanting.* How much longer could she stay celibate in that small tent alone with a powerful, sexy, rain-drenched Dylan MacCabe? Playing fish. Backgammon. Pretending to read by the light of a flashlight, with Dylan's warmth filling up the tent. She'd long given up telling him her travel stories. She couldn't stand having him stare at her for so long. They lived in such intimacy…yet they weren't intimate enough.

She opened her eyes and shrugged the weight of the pack against her shoulders. She tried to concentrate on her breathing. She tried to put herself in the athlete's mind-set. As if she were on the fifth mile of a six-mile run, and had set her heart on breaking her own personal record. Don't complain. Work yourself to the bone. Never do less than your very best. Go the extra mile. Work through the pain.

Work through the pain.

She felt the strange bite of tears at the backs of her eyes. She blinked, hard, to make them go away. She'd spent three years working through the pain. She wasn't ready for this. She simply wasn't ready for this.

She stubbed her foot against an upraised root. Dylan stopped and glanced back at her. He looked—dripping wet and all—like an advertisement for hiking boots.

"You all right back there?"

Flat and unemotional. No gentleness. No real concern. A droplet fell from above and splashed on the tip of her nose.

She fixed her gaze on the ground so he would not see her tears.

"Yeah, Dylan." She shoved her thumb under the shoulder of her backpack. "I'm doing just fine."

An hour later Dylan reached the summit of a granite promontory that jutted out into the curve of the river. From this vantage point, he could see the whole expanse of the wild countryside, the tips of the firs, the rounded humps of bare rock heaving up, here and there, from the forest; the silver thread of the stream they followed, winding amid the wispy fog. He dropped his pack on the rock and climbed a jutting needle of rock to search for the Owl's Head promontory.

He peered up and down the river. He pulled out his binoculars, and scanned the same territory. He cursed the fog and leaned out perilously far. It had to be here somewhere. It had to be. According to his calculations he should be right on top of it. And before they traveled any farther he had to find it, for all his calculations to the portages depended on pinpointing the location of Owl's Head Rock.

Finally he climbed back down from the slippery needle of rock, flipped open the laminated map, and sank to his haunches.

It was no use. He'd gone over the calculations again and again. The landmark should be here, and he couldn't find it anywhere. The frustration was getting to him.

Frustration seemed to be the emotion of the day.

He glanced over to the source of that emotion. Casey leaned against a rock with her eyes closed and her face lifted to the mist. That stubborn kid was wearing herself out. They were behind schedule. He had no choice but to push her—but he was pushing too hard.

Then she swiped a hank of hair off her brow. Her wet T-shirt pulled tight against her breast, showing, through the thin fibers, the dark peak of a tight areola. All his pretense that she was nothing but a kid fluttered away with the rising wind.

She caught his eye. Their gazes locked for a moment. Then, abruptly, she lowered her arm and hiked up a knee to cover her breast.

"So, Lewis," she said, "have we found the mouth of the Mississippi yet?"

"Not yet." He shook out his dripping laminated map and rolled it up tight. "But we've got to be close."

"So we're still lost."

He gave her a look, but all she did was cast him a weary little smile.

"I've thought of something," she said, running her fingers through her slicked-back hair. "I've been thinking about it all the way up here. I do my best thinking when I'm running, you know."

He hiked his hands onto his hips, eyeing her, eyeing that weary little smile and feeling more than a little twinge of guilt for pushing her so hard. "So, what is it?"

"I don't know if you want to hear it," she said, with an airy wave of her hand, "you being so sure of your directions and all."

"Casey..."

"When I look at that map, I see it in a different way than you, Dylan."

He cocked a brow at her. He would be angry if the idea weren't so ludicrous. He'd spent years studying this map. He'd spent almost as long searching through sources for further information about the old trading routes. He'd stared at this map so much that he knew it by heart.

"All right, Clark," he said. "Is this some kind of female-intuition thing? What other way is there to look at this?"

"When that Frenchman made that map," she said, raising her other knee and tucking them both under her chin, "didn't you tell me he made it for other Frenchmen, looking to sell furs to the English?"

"Yeah."

"Then he made the map to sell to men planning to come south, right?"

"Yeah, so?"

He stilled the urge to wince. He knew he sounded testy. Demanding. Not at all like a patient teacher of overactive sixteen- to-eighteen-year-old students. If she'd been sixteen, he could have handled it. But this was a woman sitting in front of him, from her plastered cap of wet hair all the way down to those long, shapely legs. A woman he'd slept next to, in a state of absolute sexual readiness, for a very, very long week.

"We're going north. Generally speaking," she added as he opened his mouth to protest. "We're taking the route into Canada, while old Henri designed this map for people coming to the States *from* Canada."

He paused, his gaze upon her, trying to concentrate on her words instead of the way her shorts gaped to give him a glimpse of smooth, tanned flesh and the crotch of her white cotton underwear.

"My read of that map says we're looking for these signs in the wrong direction." She gestured to the rock Dylan was leaning against, and then looked up at the rock she was leaning against. "Heck, we could be sitting right on top of old Owl's Head Rock."

He stood from his crouch as her words sank in. He flipped open the curled map. He looked ahead on the map; he looked behind, to ground they'd already passed. He noticed where Henri had put the markings. Then he snapped the map into a roll and backed away from the rock he'd been leaning against. He looked around at the top of the promontory, noticing for the first time the two large jutting needles of rock, one closer to the river, the other set farther back.

Then with a clamber of footsteps he headed down the opposite descent of the promontory. He heard the scrape of her sneakers as she followed. He stopped when they got a few feet down to look back up, at the rock formations. He clambered still lower, through the spindly tough trunks of trees with their roots dug into the rock, and stopped to stare up again. He noticed the two pointed rocks set on an angle at either end of the promontory—rocks that would be concealed from the river coming from the south, but would look very much like owl's ears, if the trees were smaller, coming from the north.

Dylan stood there staring at the rock formation, with the mist breathing down upon his face, and his own breath coming fast, watching Casey pause just ahead of him and arch her long neck to look up at the rock formation. Then she turned with the most unbearable look of triumph in her dancing brown eyes.

The lady was right. They'd been sitting on Owl's Head Rock all along. And he'd been too blind to see it—or too preoccupied with a certain sexy brunette to think straight.

"So," she said, planting her fists on her hips and herself right in front of him. "What does Davy Crockett have to say now about female intuition and a fresh perspective?"

There was a lot he could think of saying, standing there staring down at her, at that jutting chin, at those dancing eyes, at the look of triumph she wore on her wet face, despite the rain dripping off her nose, despite the smudge of dirt across her shirt.

Instead, he just shrugged and with a rising grin said, "I told you we weren't lost."

She gasped, her mouth gaped open, and with an incredulous laugh she slapped him on the arm. "You!" She slapped him again, on the other arm. "The arrogance of men! I can't believe—"

"It was just a matter of time," he said, veering away from the flail of her arms, "before I would have noticed we were sitting right on top of it."

"If I hadn't said anything," she argued, "we'd have been looking all day—"

"Not on your life—"

"Isn't that like a man," she gasped, "taking credit when none is due! Admit it, Dylan, admit that I was right."

"It was certainly wise of you to point out—"

"No, none of that!" she exclaimed, waving a finger in front of his face. "Say it. Say, 'Casey, you were right.'"

"Hey, you weren't the only one—"

"What, is it a genetic defect? A man can't admit when someone else is right?"

"Okay, all right." He caught a flailing arm and softened his voice. "Casey, you were right. One-hundred-percent right."

Then, after a silence, they laughed, both of them, aloud and to each other. They laughed, her hand caught in his, as the gray mist of mid-morning hazed down among the trees...and it was as if a great tense spring had unwound between them.

He watched the spread of her smile and thought that he preferred her like this—open, bright-eyed, alive, full of teasing. He hadn't heard her laugh in days. Since before that morning in the cove when he'd been so foolish as to sink his soapy fingers into her hair and taste her lips. There had been ease between them before—a sweet and new friendship—an easy, simple partnership; and standing here now in the wet litter of a wild forest, he wanted that easy friendship with her with a new and sudden fierceness.

As soon as the thought formed, another came hard upon it. For no sooner had the laughter started than it began to fade. Her fingers tensed, then curled in his. The bright light in her eyes mellowed into something different, a soft gleam that spoke not of easy friendship and simple partnerships, but of a relationship far deeper and far more dangerous.

Around them the rain pattered on the leaves and dripped off the pine needles to scent the air with sap and resin. It seemed that they were so very alone. So very far from civilization. Yet he knew they either stood on public ground, or they'd drifted into one of the large privately-owned estates in the Adirondacks that he'd gotten permission to cross. Any moment now, they could run into a park ranger or a private groundskeeper.

Yet, under these pines he felt as primitive, as primeval as the old forest around them. He wanted to strip off her clothes and make love to her on the wet forest floor.

The tight coil that had so swiftly unwound tensed up between them just as quickly.

There would be no easy friendship with this woman. Dylan knew, staring into those amber eyes, that nothing would be easy between them again. Yet before them lay two weeks of hard travel, alone, with no distractions but each other and the voyage; two weeks of telling himself that he would play the gentleman because she'd made her choice. She'd rebuffed him at the cove, for reasons he still did not understand, reasons that had something to do with a mysterious husband.

What the hell was he thinking, anyway? Friendship and sexual attraction were a potent, dangerous mix. That problem had gotten him married twice before, and exploded in his face. The last thing he needed was to make love to a woman he admired and enjoyed spending time with. The last thing he needed was the makings of another wife.

He didn't think his ego—or his heart—could take another ruined relationship. He didn't think he could start dreaming of home and family and watch the image implode before it could be realized.

He dropped her hand. He tightened his own hands into fists. She was staring as still and silent as the oak at her back while rivers of emotion flowed through her eyes. Moments passed, marked only by the patter of rain.

From the distance came a rumble of thunder. Around them, the patter of rain intensified.

"Come on," he said, hearing his own voice hoarse and tense. "We'd best get the tent up before the storm hits us good."

IT WAS GOING TO HAPPEN. Casey felt it in her bones, in her blood. They were going to make love—tonight.

They worked in an uneasy silence, tapping in the tent

poles and stretching the tarp over the frame of the tent, while the mist-turned-to-rain turned into a steady downpour. Casey fussed with the packs in the canoe longer than she needed to, standing knee-deep in water and delaying the moment when she would have to bend under the flap of that tent and be alone inside it with Dylan.

She tugged her pack out of the tight space between keel and seat, then heaved it onto her shoulder. With one reddened hand she struggled to pull the tarp tight over the floating canoe. The water lapped against her knees, but she hardly noticed it anymore. She hardly noticed any discomforts—the water soaking her hair, the chill of the coming storm, the blackness of the sky. Her senses, her body were numb to all but the man waiting in the tent.

It is going to happen...tonight.

She told herself that she couldn't do this. Dylan was a stranger. She'd made Charlie wait two years before she had let him lure her into the back seat of his father's car, and by then they were all but engaged. She couldn't just climb into that tent and let Dylan touch her body so intimately, after only a week or so of knowing him. She just wasn't the type to have a fling with a stranger.

It was embarrassing how little experience she had in a situation like this, a woman of her age, in these days. She'd taken lovemaking seriously all her life—she'd never even had a casual affair. But Dylan had had two wives, and was lighthearted enough about the divorces. He was an experienced man and she was nothing but a nervous half-virgin, for goodness' sake.

She should be thankful for that, at least. Dylan would want nothing but a fling, and that was more than she could handle. Any more serious relationship was simply too terrifying to contemplate.

Then the flap of the tent flew open and he stuck out his

head to yell above the rain. "C'mon, Casey, the heavens are going to open any minute now."

"I'll...I'll be right there."

The flap fell down. She finished tightening the tarp and curled her fingers around the strap of her overnight pack. She took a deep, cleansing breath and looked up, past the shooting trunks of the pines, to the ferment of the blackening sky.

I'm not ready for this. The rain pattered on her skin. *It's going to happen...tonight.*

Dylan was rubbing his hair briskly with a towel when she splashed into the tent. He didn't raise his head when she entered. He'd thrown on a fresh, dry shirt, but he'd neglected to button it. She tore her gaze away from his washboard abdomen.

She tossed her pack into her corner, crouched down and started peeling off wet clothes. With her back to him, she peeled off each layer and tossed the wet garments into a corner. When she got to her T-shirt and shorts, she lost courage and seized a towel.

She draped the towel across her shoulders and showed him her back. She could hear him breathing as she wiggled out of her bra and shimmied out of her underwear. She could feel his gaze upon her wet hair, upon her back. The nylon floor of the tent chilled her buttocks. She fumbled, one-handed, in her pack, seeking fresh undergarments. She waited for him to approach. Wondering when his shadow would fall over her...when he would kneel behind her...when she would feel his lips on her skin...on her breasts.

She curled her hand over her undergarments. Then, awkwardly, she slipped one leg then the other into her panties. She shimmied them up, rising to pull them over her buttocks. She could hear every rustle he made. She jumped at every catch in his breathing.

She squeezed her eyes shut. When was he going to touch her? She didn't know whether she dreaded his approach or anticipated it; emotions roiled in her body, too many and too confused to sort. She slipped the straps of her bra over her arms and leaned forward, fumbling with the clasp. Her breasts tingled, felt heavy in the cups. She couldn't seem to clasp it and finally, she whipped off the bra and tossed it aside.

Still, he didn't move. She sensed his stillness behind her. She heard his intake of breath when the towel slipped off one of her shoulders as she was reaching for a dry T-shirt. She yanked the T-shirt over her head, then, with nervous hands, she snapped the towel off her shoulders and buried her wet head in it.

She pressed her fingers into the towel to stop them from trembling. Her whole body was trembling. She didn't know how much more of this she could take.

Then she heard the sound of playing cards being skill-fully shuffled.

She twisted around and lifted the towel. She met his gaze across the glare of the hanging lantern. He looked weary. Vaguely amused. And full of the knowledge that this was going to be a difficult afternoon for both of them—yet again.

"Let's see," he said, shuffling the cards from one hand to another. "Where did we leave off? Two-to-one in gin rummy—my advantage. Feel like making it three out of five?"

She let the towel slide to her lap. His gaze drifted to her wet hair, then down her body, only to skitter back to the cards in his hands.

"'Course," he continued, "I completely pummeled you

in gin rummy. We could start over with that game, if you think you can take another drubbing."

She stared at him as he shuffled, leaning so casually with one elbow on the ground and his long legs stretched out, his shirt hanging open, a half smile on his craggy face. Only his eyes showed the cost of this supposed casualness—blue and bright and hungry—and, but for a brief moment, hooded from her sight.

He wasn't going to make a move on her. He wasn't going to make love to her. Not for lack of desire—she could see that clearly enough—but for some other reason.... Some sweet and deferential reason; some kind and wary reason.

Something warm lit in her belly, a strange sort of heated glow that filled her so full that she couldn't find the words to speak.

"So, what d'you say, hmm?" He held up the deck. "It's the lady's choice."

She shook her head, slowly.

"No?" He split the pack to shuffle it again. "What, do you want backgammon instead?"

"No, no," she murmured, feeling as if she were sliding down a slippery slope with no chance of catching herself from her own folly.

Oh, she was crazy. It must be the bad food. Maybe she was getting feverish from so many days in the damp. This was pure, unadulterated folly. She definitely, definitely was not ready for this.

Then she met his gaze and let herself tumble.

"Dylan... How about strip poker?"

8

THE CARDS SPRAYED OUT of his hands, flipped in a wild arc, batted against the roof of the tent, then rained down upon them. Casey's words reverberated in the air. She sat steady amid the fluttering cards, her gaze fixed upon Dylan's. A wonderful calm settled over her. Like the day she'd finally sold the house she and Charlie had lived in. A sense of letting go...a feeling of total freedom.

This is the right choice, she told herself, as Dylan pushed himself up from his reclining position. *This is the right thing to do.* Jillian was right. This must be part of the healing process. She was a grown woman in the 1990s, old enough to know the difference between love and sex. Dylan was a good man, a steady man—he'd just proved that to her. He would end this well.

But then all thought washed out of her head, for Dylan loomed across the space that separated them, knocking the lantern so that it swung wildly, shooting shadows across the tent. He raked his hand through her hair and yanked her head back. The rough calluses of his fingers scraped against her scalp.

Then he sealed her lips with a kiss.

This kiss bore no resemblance to that teasing, wet kiss of the cove. It was a kiss that spoke of hunger and little gentleness. She swayed with the force of it and braced her hands on the ground behind her.

When he finally tore away, he held her fast and said, "Say it again, Casey."

She blinked up into those fierce Viking eyes and tried to stop her senses from swimming. "Wh-what?"

"The card game. What you want to play." His fingers flexed in her hair. "Because once the cards get dealt, there's no folding."

"I'm not folding." She straightened and curled her fingers around the edges of his open shirt. "I want to play strip poker," she whispered, peeling the edges of the shirt apart, her heart racing at her own boldness. "Winner take all."

Then she lost the capacity to breathe as she stretched his shirt wide. There was something innately dangerous about the sight of a man's naked chest. Especially when the man involved was wide-shouldered, small-waisted, and finely chiseled—from the strong slash of collarbone all the way down to the none-too-gentle ripples of his abdomen. And so big. So dangerously big. So breathtakingly powerful.

She'd seen him without a shirt before. But never at such close range. Close enough to lean forward and slip the tip of her tongue over the hollow of his chest.

No sooner had the thought shocked her than she'd already done it. He tasted of rainwater. His skin felt surprisingly smooth, the whorls of gold-tipped hair soft against her lips.

He made a rumbling noise deep in his chest and clasped her upper arms in a tight grip.

"Cheater," he accused as he set her away. "You're not playing fair. You haven't shown me your hand yet."

Then, so quickly that it was done before she could think, he gathered her T-shirt at the waist and yanked it over her head. He balled up the shirt and sent it flying to the corner of the tent, and then she was sitting before him, naked from the waist up.

No man had laid eyes upon her body for years, and now she sat with her breath caught in her throat and the glare of the swinging lantern on her skin as Dylan touched her with his gaze so hungrily that her nipples tightened. He watched, a muscle flexing in his cheek. A blush crept up to tingle her skin.

"A pair of aces," he murmured. "And me, with an empty hand."

He filled one of his empty hands with the weight of her breast. He scraped his thumb, ever-so-lightly, against the engorged peak. She couldn't help it—the motion was instinctive—she arched her back as the rush of sensation shot through her, which drove her breast deeper into the warm, moist palm of his hand.

When the blindness ebbed she found him watching her intensely, hunger plain in his eyes. And her body moved of its own accord, finding his hardness and warmth rising beneath the soft cloth of his sweatpants.

Then it came to her in all its carnal glory, what they were to do in this tent on this night. The expectation sent a whole new rush of sensation through her.

She did not reel back. She did not hesitate. In some distant part of her mind, she knew she should be shocked by her own boldness. It was as if some strange woman had taken over her body; she couldn't believe the things she was thinking, the things she was doing, like right now, as she curled her hand tightly around his erection, and felt the pulse of pleasure shoot through his body.

When she spoke, her voice was but a whisper. "Haven't you ever played five-card stud, Dylan? This is no empty hand—this is very definitely a straight."

His teeth flashed in the light of the lantern, and he moved

his mouth closer to hers. "And you, my bold Casey, have a royal flush."

She managed a shaky smile. "I win, then."

"We both win," he murmured, as he dipped his face into her throat. "And the game has just begun."

He pressed her down. Her spine softened as she sank to the slippery carpet of cards. It all rushed in on her; the welcome slap of his weight, the heat of bare skin grazing bare skin, the spicy-hot still on his tongue. She wound her arms around his shoulders. His lips met hers. Hard. Catching her gasp. And he worked her mouth and her tongue and her lips until she was starved for him, until she reached up to meet him with each kiss.

Then he broke the contact and she lay back, gasping for air and for something else, something much more substantial. He kissed her jaw and her throat, and lower, lower, to graze the stubble of his cheek against the peak of her breast.

She clawed her fingers into his shirt, and wondered why she had waited so long for something that felt so right. So perfect. His head...it fit in her hands. He felt so warm atop her. Their naked skins slipped so sweetly, one against the another. It had been so long, but she knew she couldn't write this intensity off as a sex-starved body screaming for release. Dylan with his tightly muscled shoulders and his hungry mouth made her want to do things—such wild, wicked things, and one thing in particular....

Then she lost all thought as the storm battered the walls of the tent and the rain pounded out a tattoo upon the canvas and they tossed their shirts and sweatpants and undergarments upon the nylon floor, and all that was left was the scent of pine and rain and the whisper of waxed cards slipping beneath their bodies.

And his hands, everywhere at once, probing between her

legs without hesitation, without gentleness, and she pressing her teeth into his shoulder as the wanting surged.

The games were over, Casey knew that. She couldn't seem to catch her breath, she couldn't think. Amid the hungry swirl of sensation he lifted himself high atop her and she felt him, the root of him, throbbing against her thigh. She let her legs fall open, welcoming him, wanting him. Just as he was about to push into her a rational thought broke through the chaos of her senses and she jerked away.

"Wait. Oh, wait!"

He stilled. She lay there, staring at him while her breath came fast through her lips. He looked as dazed as she, as anxious as she felt. She struggled to her elbows and pushed up, away from him, away from that dangerous, pulsating strength. "Wait," she breathed. "I'm not... We can't... We have to... Oh, *hell!*"

She glanced toward her pack, just within arm's reach. What was she supposed to say? She didn't know how to do this. When she was last in this situation she was in the back of Charlie's father's car and she was seventeen years old. She made an awkward lunge for her pack and the protection it contained.

"Casey," he said, slapping a hand on her hip. "I've—"

"One minute," she said, yanking the zipper open. "Just one minute. I've got... Right here."

She closed her fingers over the box. She pulled it out, wiggled back down and held it before her—just as Dylan yanked his own box out of his backpack and held it up.

For a moment they lay in silence, their skins hot and close, their breath coming fast, while they held two identical purple boxes up at each other. For a heartbeat the rain sounded very loud against the tarpaulin. They lay there, bodies entwined, holding the same brand of condoms.

Then Casey smiled and heard Dylan's soft, shaky laughter that rumbled through his body and found an echo in her own. With that sexy laughter came a rush of relief—for now there would be no awkward conversations, no discussions of safety and birth control, no onus on her to talk him into wearing one instead of doing what they both wanted to do—plunge hot turgid skin into soft moist flesh and consequences be damned. With that sexy laughter came a sense of peace...and trust.

"Same brand," Dylan said, as his heated smile lingered. "Both lubricated, too."

She reached up and rubbed her fingers against the bristle on his cheek. "I should have known you'd have one, Mr. Ever Ready."

"I bought them two days after I met you, lady." His voice deepened. "I didn't expect you'd have a box of your own."

She felt her color deepen. She'd bought them while she was buying camera batteries and a few other essentials at the drugstore before they'd left. In a moment of folly almost as crazed as this. On a whim... Or maybe it had been a moment of premonition.

She held his gaze but could not find the words to speak. They were going deep. Maybe too deep, and she didn't want to think about such things. Not now.

She settled down on the cool nylon floor. She let her box drop to her side as he dealt with the necessaries. She watched him fit the latex over himself, and found the sight fascinating...and exciting...for soon he would be rolling himself into *her*.

He nudged her legs apart, then surged atop her, his skin rasping against hers, as he braced his forearms on either side of her. He kissed her—no, it was more like a bite. He ridged his teeth against the line of her jaw as she arched up, so her nipples scraped the hair on his chest. His thighs felt

rough against the tender flesh of her own inner thighs—
and he felt hot, probing her hard.

"Casey… I've wanted you for so long—"

"Oh…" She caught her lower lip between her teeth as he
pushed deeper. "Dylan…"

She grasped the muscles of his back as her whole body
flexed around him; they fit, oh, how they fit, and it seemed
to Casey that she lost a part of herself every time Dylan
drew back for a stroke. She clasped him closer, stretched
her hands up to his head and raked her fingers through his
damp hair. The moisture of the rain, the moisture of their
bodies, made their skins slick against one another, made
her feel all the more one body with this muscle-bound lover
she'd chosen for reasons she no longer cared to examine.

For the movement between them loosed a wild part of
herself, loosed a sensuous creature of instinct who arched,
and arched again, to meet him, to draw him deeper, to
reach that thrumming quiver of glorious forgetfulness so
that, for a few dazzling moments, they could revel—together—in the purest, most intimate joy of all.

Later, long after they were both still, she became aware
of the patter of the rain upon the tent, and the bowing of the
wind against the walls. Wet waxed cards clung to her back,
and hot male skin molded against her hips and thighs.

She opened her eyes dreamily. Dylan was watching her,
his face inches from hers. A lock of his hair, long dried, fell
over his forehead. She resisted the urge to reach up and
sweep it back; she liked that he looked boyish. She liked the
soft, strange smile playing about his mouth. She liked that
he had not yet lifted himself off her, that he toyed with a
strand of her hair.

Already…already she felt a yearning for him again.

Her gaze fell, briefly, upon the open purple box on its
side beside them. "Do you think," she whispered, tilting

her head toward the debris, "that we'll have enough of those until we reach civilization?"

"Hell," he murmured in a shaky voice, lowering his lips to hers. "I was just wondering if we'll have enough for tonight."

MORNING DAWNED BRIGHT and wet. Dylan flung the tarp of the tent aside and climbed out into the glory of nature wearing nothing but a yawn. Rainbows sparkled in the water dripping off the trees. He swaggered to the edge of the river, filled his lungs with the scent of the late-summer air, and resisted the urge to run like hell.

Casey...

Sensual images of the night flooded through his mind, generating an instant rise in him. The downy feel of her earlobe in his mouth. The tender sensitivity of the white flesh of her thighs. The firmness of the curve of her hip. The way she moaned when he scraped his tongue across her breast. The hot, womanly taste of her sex.

He raked his hands through his hair, then curled his fingers into fists. They'd made love over and over last night, each time more hungrily, more fiercely, than the last. He'd forgotten how good a woman could feel. He'd forgotten the mind-numbing pleasure of it all.

He shook his head. What a lousy liar he was. He hadn't forgotten a damned thing. He hadn't been a saint since his last divorce. But last night had little to do with lust. Casey had felt *right* lying by his side, in a way more fundamental than any woman had ever felt before. The way she'd moved, the way she'd cried out when she'd climaxed, the sweet smell of the nape of her neck, the way she'd spooned her body around his when it was all over...

It had never been like that before. Never.

He crouched down by the river, let his fingers slide

through his hair, and buried his head between his elbows. What the hell was he doing? What the hell had he gotten himself into? Why couldn't he make love to a woman and leave it at that? He was darn near forty years old. He'd grown comfortable in his bachelorhood. He took great pleasure in his weekend fishing trips to the cabin that his married friends couldn't take without checking first with the wife. And he'd tried the married life before. Twice before. One wild night under the stars with Casey and he was already thinking of white lace and wedding vows.

Damn it. Not this time. Not this time. He was going to enjoy an uncomplicated relationship with a beautiful woman. He was sure of one thing: Come the end of this camping trip, Casey Michaels was going to climb back into her minivan and set off for destinations unknown, leaving him behind.

He would be a fool to let her leave him behind with a broken heart.

He plunged his hands into the river, then splashed his face with cold water. Again. And again. Until rivulets slipped over his chin, down his neck, to soak his chest. He raked his wet hands through his hair, soaking it to his head, welcoming the chill of the morning to cool the heat of his thoughts. Rising up, he stepped into the cold river up to his thighs, then dived in to swim until his body and his thoughts chilled.

Later, much later, when his body had dried and he'd made coffee and breakfast, he pulled on a pair of dry shorts and muscled up the will to enter the tent.

He braced himself, then flung open the tarp. The air inside the tent was thick with the scent of woman, with the scent of sex. The misty light of dawn fell upon a figure huddled under the sleeping bag. The figure rolled over, and a pair of wary brown eyes peeked over the flannel edge of the sleeping bag.

"Dylan?" She winced against the hazy light as she struggled up. "Is it dawn already?"

"Almost."

He said the word in a strangled voice, for the sleeping bag slipped down to reveal one pert, perfectly formed breast. The tarp fell out of his fingers, plunging them both into an intimate dimness.

She lowered her hand from her eyes but made no move to cover herself. She looked strangely vulnerable this morning, with her hair mussed, her eyes heavy with sleep, and all traces of lipstick kissed off her lips. Not at all like the well-dressed, self-confident journalist who had breezed into his life not so long ago. Not at all like the competent, courageous woman who was his partner in this crazy adventure.

She looked one-hundred-percent woman. Soft. Vulnerable. Lovely. Incredibly sexy. And full of the knowledge of her own power over him. This was the side of her that threatened to bring him to his knees.

Literally.

"I made coffee," he said. His voice sounded rough to his own ears. "Breakfast, too."

"A man who makes breakfast the morning after. A rare and precious find." She ran her fingers through her unkempt hair, making her breast rise and pucker. "How about eggs and bacon, Dylan? French toast and fresh-squeezed orange juice?"

"How about oatmeal?"

She grimaced. "How romantic."

"I'll feed it to you."

She stilled. Their eyes met. His gaze dipped to her breast,

and he thought of all the possibilities inherent in spoons and warm oatmeal and two willing bodies.

"Dylan," she said, in a voice more breath than sound, "you have a wicked side."

He had to get out of here. He pushed out the tarp. "Are you coming for breakfast?"

"Later." She sank back down in the sleeping bag. "I lost track of the poker game last night," she said, as she tucked one hand under her pillow. "Do you remember who was winning?"

He felt the blood rush out of his head, and converge in his hardening loins. "The bank," he said, jerking his head toward a little plastic bag that held the neatly rubber-packed evidence of their nocturnal activities. "It's making a fortune off us."

"How about you and me making another deposit?"

His jaw tightened. He stared at her soft little smile, at the breast winking at him, at the stretch of her side and the leg she'd slipped around the sleeping bag.

Then he was kneeling at her side, peeling the sleeping bag off her body, close enough to feel her warmth, close enough to see the flex of her soft belly, to see her nipple tighten into a sensitive little knot.

She had exquisitely sensitive nipples—only one of the wonders he'd discovered about her body last night. So he leaned over her and scraped his cheek against her breast, then took the hard nub gently between his teeth.

She sucked in a breath and convulsed beneath him. He tugged her nipple, and teased the throbbing tip with his tongue, closing his eyes as her body spoke to his.

He listened. He did as she wished. He ran his fingers down into the damp cleft between her legs, rubbing the tiny nub until she made that strangled little noise in her throat. He settled himself heavily upon her, welcomed the embrace of her arms, welcomed that other, more intimate embrace. He stroked into her darkness, hovering on the edge of losing all control, until she dug her fingers into his back and convulsed around him, crying out his name—and then he let himself fall.

After he'd drained his passion into her once again, he rose up and looked deep into those smoky brown eyes. And felt himself getting caught in them. Stuck fast. Like a fly in amber.

DYLAN NUDGED THE GEAR to make sure it was packed tightly into the canoe, then tugged each of the ropes for tautness. The sun beat hot upon his back. He and Casey had whiled away half the morning, and it was long past time they were back on the trail.

Rising from his work, he glimpsed Casey sitting on the shore. Her head was bent over her tattered journal, and her pen flew across the page. Her wet hair gleamed with chestnut highlights where the sun hit it through the webbing of trees.

"So," he said, marching to the shore, "I'll bet that journal has just gotten very interesting."

She glanced up. Her pen stilled. A smile spread across her lips, painted with a slick coat of that mysterious brown lipstick. "Now, Dylan, do you really think I'd write down *all* the juicy details?"

"You are a journalist," he said. "A slave to fact."

"Yes, fact," she said, flattening the pages against her chest as he leaned over to try to see them. "So that's what I've written—fact. A record of where we've gone, what we've seen, how long it has taken—"

"Uh-huh."

A wicked gleam lit her eye. Dylan felt the now familiar

sinking sensation in his loins, and wondered how much a man and a woman could make love before collapsing.

"If you have to know, Dylan, I was just recording some important survival details for anyone else wanting to make this trip."

"Oh, yeah? Like what?"

"Well, for one," she said, "I've included the many unintended-but-intriguing uses for oatmeal."

He felt the spread of a slow grin. He'd scrubbed well after their sticky breakfast, but he was sure he would find flakes of oatmeal in his hair for days. "You should see what I can do with peanut butter."

"Dylan!"

"I hope you're intending to write up that experience for some other market," he said. "*Playboy*, perhaps. Or *Penthouse*?"

She shook her head. "Too tame. Need a racier magazine." She pursed her lips. "I suppose I could call it 'Three and a Half Weeks' or 'My Days with a Wild Mountain Man.'"

"Wild mountain man?"

"I did warn you that anything you say or do could be used against you—"

"Against me? Hell, a story like this would do wonders for my reputation around Bridgewater."

"You know, I'm beginning to think you made all that up." She lumbered to her feet and tucked the journal into her backpack, then pressed her lean body against his and wrapped her arms around his neck. "There isn't a boring bone in your very marvelous body, Dylan MacCabe."

"I'm glad you think so."

He kept smiling down into those bright brown eyes, and kept his hands firm on her hips, but inside he felt his smile wither. Ah, yes, the sun was bright on his back, the air was fresh, and desire sang in the veins of them both, but this was a moment out of time. Casey couldn't imagine who he really was—not here, not now.

But that was okay, he told himself. For it was sure she wouldn't be hanging around after the trip was over. There had been no talk of the future. It didn't matter if she imagined him a wild mountain man, for she would never know the high-school history teacher who lived in a backwater town and loved it.

"C'mon," he said, stepping away. "If we keep this up, we'll never make it to the end of this trip."

They paddled through most of the morning. Though the sun blazed bright on the water and the birds sang joyous music in the trees around them, he felt as if a dark cloud hung over him. She tried a few times to tease him into banter, but he didn't have the tongue for it. They soon fell silent.

It should have been a companionable silence. All this past week or so, they'd managed to paddle together without filling the silence between them with words. That was yet another thing he liked about Casey—she understood the silence necessary for concentration, even physical concentration. She understood the athlete's mind-set. There weren't a heck of a lot of women he knew who did.

But this, for the first time, was not an easy silence between them. And Dylan wasn't such an insensitive brute that he couldn't recognize the uneasiness. He supposed that two people who had just slept together would usually get to separate into their own worlds for a while just about now, to reassess the situation away from their new lover... To have time to wonder if it had been a wise decision to sleep together; time to grapple with any confusion over the state of this fragile new relationship. But he and Casey were not afforded such a luxury. He knew they would be together, inseparable, for ten days to two weeks more. And so between them swam a river of confusion and unspoken, unspeakable questions.

Part of him wanted to steer the canoe to the nearest riverbank and drown the awkwardness between them in a healthy bout of lovemaking. But this voyage beckoned, and they were behind schedule, and they'd already spent half a morning exploring each other's bodies—and no doubt would do the same when they broke for lunch.

Besides...he wasn't so sure that would help the situation. The more time he spent with Casey, the more he wanted to spend time with Casey. He was falling too hard, too fast.

As usual.

So he lost himself in the physical exertion, and they covered six miles in record time. Then they both started looking for the next marker on the map—a portage to another stream. They scanned the northwest bank of the river for a break in the greenery.

They paddled a mile farther, then backtracked, closer to the river's edge. Dylan used his paddle to push away the overgrowth. Finally, they found a sliver of riverbank free of greenery that seemed to extend inward.

"Are you sure this is it?" Casey asked, frowning over the well-marked map on her lap. "It doesn't look like much of a path."

"It's got to be. There's nothing else around here. Anything we find would be overgrown, anyway."

"Yeah, but I'd expect it to have some kind of marking."

"A break in the trees, Casey. That's the marking."

He hadn't told Casey yet, but they'd reached the most confusing part of the route. The part for which Henri had left the least information, the least definitive markings—and the part where the webbing of rivers and the depth of the woods were at their thickest. Of course, she probably had figured that out on her own, judging by the way she was squinting at the map. But he didn't want to worry her. She seemed to have a terrible fear of getting lost.

They splashed out of the canoe and into the shallows. Dylan secured it to a branch and they started unloading.

After they'd spread the gear on dry land, he helped her strap on the frame of the backpack they would be using to carry the gear over the portages. He pulled the straps tight over her shoulders. His fingers lingered on her collarbone; it looked so fragile, jutting from her skin. Not strong enough to hold her head, the sweep of her shimmering brown hair—never mind thirty pounds of weight in a backpack.

Then his gaze caught hers, and there he saw questions. Confusion. Curiosity. And a host of other emotions he couldn't quite name.

Yeah, he was acting strangely. She was making him feel strange. Protective. Lusty.

He let his hand drop from her throat. "Don't take too much weight, Casey," he warned. "It could be a long portage."

"Hey, we're back in my territory now," she said, shrugging. "Dry land. I'm a runner, remember? This I can handle."

He let his gaze wander down over those long, tanned legs and tried not to imagine them bent across his back. She caught his glance and a hesitant smile quirked her lips.

"You know," she said softly, "I thought that once we'd made love, you'd stop acting like a cranky bear."

He choked. "A cranky bear?"

"Yeah. You've been grunting all the way from our last campsite." She tilted her head and examined him. "I thought...making love...would ease things between us."

"Well," he admitted, "it eased something."

"I'll say."

"Is that why you did it?" he asked abruptly. "To put me in a better mood?"

He wished he could bite back the words, but there they were, reverberating between them. She looked surprised. Uncertain. He could have kicked himself. What did it matter why she'd made love to him? He wasn't looking for happily-ever-after. And, he suspected, neither was she.

"Because...I wanted to." Her smile softened, grew hesitant. "And because...you're a good man, Dylan."

Something inside him shifted...moved. With a dangerous sliding sensation. *You're a good man, Dylan.* He searched her eyes. He dug his fingers into the softness of her hair. Yeah, he was a "good man." A "nice guy." He'd once been told he had a "good shoulder," too. In his experience, nice guys always finished last.

He dropped his hands. He stepped away from her. He needed to focus. On the trip. Not on Casey. Not on this thing building between them.

"C'mon, Case." He rolled his shoulders. "We'd best get going or we'll never make it home by September."

She shifted the weight on her back and eyed the thickness of the forest. "You brought your machete, I trust?"

"No. Remember, take only pictures, leave—"

"Only footprints." She wrinkled her nose. "I know."

"It won't be so bad," he told her. "I'll lead."

"Uh, Dylan... Are you sure there aren't any wild animals in there?"

"Only the two-legged type." He waggled his brows at her, which was about as much levity as he was capable of. "C'mon, Casey. The sooner we find the next stream, the sooner we can have lunch."

She perked up. "Lunch? What's for lunch?"

He couldn't resist. He flashed her an evil grin.

"Peanut butter."

CASEY TRUDGED AFTER Dylan as the sun slanted long shadows through the trees. After seven hours of portaging back and forth and around and about, thirty pounds of weight felt more like a hundred upon her back. The straps dug deep into her shoulders and sweat bathed her shirt between the shoulder blades, though a cool evening breeze had started to sway the ferns.

All day, she had felt as if she were walking on air. She'd spent the morning watching his strong back as he paddled the canoe, remembering how she'd dug her fingernails into the ridge between his shoulder blades as he'd made love to her. And when they'd first started portaging, she'd watched his legs as he walked, the pumping of his muscles, and tried not to dissolve into jelly on the forest floor. Dylan MacCabe knew how to make love to a woman, and Casey had never felt so utterly, totally satisfied.

She'd spent the day wanting him.

But as the day wore on, and they backtracked and regrouped and set off on another false trail again, her mood had darkened even as Dylan's had turned brighter and lighter. Because for all of Dylan's whistling, for all of his easy quips, nothing could dispel the knowledge tied like a knot in her gut that they were hopelessly lost in the woods.

Lost.

She hadn't been paying attention. She'd allowed herself to be distracted by him. She'd long ago lost her bearings on her copy of the map. She'd allowed herself to follow blindly, without thinking; she'd allowed him to lead and she had followed like a dull-witted duckling. And now, almost twenty-four hours after she'd chucked her misgivings about getting physically involved with him, she was quivering as if she were on the verge of a nervous breakdown.

Everything was mixed up in her mind. The lovemaking. The total release she'd felt in his presence. The sense of safety. The warmth shimmering between them. The sure, terrifying knowledge that they were lost in the wilds.

She knew better than to drop her guard, even for a little while. She knew better than to place her hope or trust or reliance in any one else's hands but her own.

"We may as well camp here," Dylan said, his voice falsely bright. "It's a good clearing, there's fresh water just over there. If we go any farther we might not find a better site."

"We should find the canoe," she argued. "At least let's find the canoe. It's has to be down river from here."

"It's ahead, but it could be a good mile or two." Dylan slipped his pack off his shoulders and let it fall to the ground. "We've walked enough for today."

"We need to find the canoe."

Dylan glanced up at her, his brow furrowing. "Casey, it's going to be dark soon. We need to pitch camp, fire up the stove, get dinner—"

"Forget dinner." She shoved her thumbs under the straps of her backpack and looked him square in the eye. "I just think...we should forge on, see if we can find our gear."

He eyed her strangely. She tried to still the quiver of her mouth. She flexed her fingers over the straps of her backpack. She met and held his gaze.

"Listen, Casey." His voice turned soft. "We have all the gear we need for the night." He patted the components of his pack. "A tent, a sleeping bag, a stove, food. You're tired, we both are. We didn't get a heck of a lot of sleep last night."

She let her gaze skid away from his. Didn't she know that well enough? Didn't she still feel the soreness between her thighs? Hadn't she spent the day in a half-dreaming state, remembering...? And in the process, he'd gotten them both lost.

"I'm not tired," she insisted. "I can walk more."

"Tomorrow."

It was a command, not a statement, and she felt herself bristle at his tone of voice.

"Tomorrow?" she repeated, knowing her voice sounded strained. "What makes you think we can find it any easier tomorrow?"

"We'll both have had a good night's sleep tomorrow."

"So? Will that make the map any clearer?"

"No. But it'll make us more clear-eyed."

"We're lost, aren't we, Dylan?"

She met his eyes squarely. She clung to his gaze, knew she was clinging to him—and hated herself for doing it. She shouldn't have gotten herself in this situation, letting herself be led around without paying attention. Now she was all turned about. She couldn't remember which direction they'd come from; she'd lost all sense of north, south, east and west. She stood as still as stone in the midst of these woods with the trees towering high above them, feeling as if she were at the center of a vortex with the world spinning around her.

"Yes, Casey," he said quietly. "We're lost."

Panic rushed through her, jolted weakness through her limbs, stole warmth from her body until she felt gooseflesh ripple her skin. *I'm lost. I'm alone.* All the world around her looked strange, and she didn't know which path would take her home.

And she knew this was foolish, she knew she was panicking over something beyond being lost in the middle of the woods, but she couldn't help herself. Everything had moved too fast for her—this relationship with Dylan, the lovemaking, and now...now this.

But *this* she could handle. They could find their way out of these woods, at least. Rescue lay in her backpack—she'd planned it that way.

She slung the pack off her shoulders, dropped to her knees, and tore at the bundles.

"Casey, listen." He stood close. Just above her. "Think of this as another experience for your story. It would have been a pretty boring piece if you hadn't gotten lost at least once—"

"You'd be surprised," she interrupted, wondering at the evenness of her voice, "how resourceful I can be when it comes to spicing up a boring story. I'd rather my adventures be fictional than real."

"Then why did you come with me?"

"I'm wondering about that myself," she muttered, yanking her overnight bag from the bottom of the pack. "You talked me into it, Dylan. You have a way of talking me into things."

"Then let me talk you into calming down."

He crouched down, placed a hand on her shoulder. Her head shot up. She stared into his face. The crinkles around his eyes, the soft comforting smile. His hand felt so warm on her skin.

How easy it would be to bury her head into that broad shoulder, to burrow within his warmth, maybe even lose herself in a few hours of lovemaking until darkness fell. Three years. Three years. She'd thought she'd learned to be self-sufficient. Now, with one night of lovemaking, she discovered she'd fallen into the same old trap—she was as weak and helpless as ever before.

She pushed away from him, thrust her hand into her bag and felt around, searching.

Dylan frowned at her. "What are you doing?"

"Looking for something." She curled her fingers over the hard block of plastic. "Here. I've got it."

She pulled out her cellular phone and prayed that it hadn't inadvertently been turned on during all the battering these packs had suffered. She prayed the batteries hadn't worn out. She flipped it open, turned it on and saw with a rush of relief the blink of the LCD.

She started pressing 9-1-1 just as Dylan seized the phone from her hands.

He glared at it as if it were some rotting animal carcass. "What the hell is this?"

"A cellular phone. I'm sure you're familiar with them, Davy Crockett."

"I know what it is. Why do you have one?"

"For just this circumstance. We're lost, Dylan. We need help."

"Like hell we do." He snapped the phone closed. "We started this trip on our own power, Casey. We're going to end it that way."

She felt a quiver deep inside her. "Oh, really? And how long will we do this? Until we're hopelessly lost? Until we can't give the search-and-rescue guys any clue as to where we are? Until the food runs out—"

"There're fish in those streams. And berries ripening in the woods." He hefted the phone in his hands, then stretched his arm back. "We sure as hell don't need this—"

"Don't!" She seized his arm, which was braced and ready to throw, stopping him from lobbing the phone deep into the darkening woods. "For God's sake, Dylan, don't!"

She reached for his hand, caught on, and clawed at his fingers until he let the phone go. He dropped it in her hands, then seized her by the shoulders.

"What is with you, Casey? I've never seen you like this."

"We're lost," she said, as if that could explain everything. "We're *lost*."

"And we'll find our way out. We're not in the Himalayas. There're no predators in these woods. We'll find our way out—together. You have to trust me."

"No."

She hadn't meant to speak, but the word lingered between them, small and mean—and truthful. For that was what it was all about, Casey realized. Trust. She didn't want to trust Dylan. Not with her body, not with her heart. She didn't want to trust anyone, anymore. And for three years she'd avoided any situation where she had to depend on another human being.

Until now.

"Casey...hell." He dug his fingers deep into her arms. "What is going on in your head? Why are you so terrified? Don't you trust me?" He shook her, hard. "Does this have something to do with that husband you won't talk about?" He must have seen something flicker in her eyes. "What the hell did he *do* to you?"

She raised her face to his and tears rose up in her throat, pushed by a swell of emotion she couldn't name, a swell of emotion she couldn't stanch, and it rose up, sticking like a ball of lead in her throat and pushing tears out of her eyes.

The words came, soft and full of sobs.

"He didn't do anything, Dylan." A tear rolled off her cheek. "He just died."

9

CASEY WRENCHED OUT OF Dylan's grip. She covered her mouth and turned away from him. She couldn't believe she'd just dropped that bomb on him. She didn't want his pity—she didn't want anyone's pity. She didn't *need* pity. She'd managed to build a whole new life for herself over these past three years and she'd put all that pain behind her.

At least, she thought she had.

"Casey...I'm sorry."

"Don't be," she said, more harshly than she intended. "It wasn't your fault. It wasn't anyone's fault. Sometimes airplanes just fall out of the sky."

The words fell so easily from her lips. She wondered if Dylan could understand how long it had taken her to admit that. It had not been an easy lesson. She'd lived such a charmed life before the accident. Somehow, Charlie's death had seemed to be her karmic payment for having lived— until then—a blissfully blessed life. Even now, her own past seemed like a dream.

No, not a dream, she told herself. A dream implied color and movement. Her old life seemed more like a print on a sparkling Christmas card—lovely, but frozen in time.

She kept her back to Dylan and hugged her elbows, then crushed her arms against her chest. Words bubbled up inside her, but she couldn't say them all at once. How could she explain how she had been, all those years before? She had been a different woman. A woman who, at the age of sixteen, had met the man she'd considered the love of her life. From that moment on, her life had followed a predictable and welcome path—attendance at a local college, marriage to the high-school sweetheart, the sacrifices to buy their little dream house, the golden retriever, the plans for children...

And it had all exploded into shards one sunny spring day, when engine failure downed a twelve-seater that Charlie had taken home from a business trip in upstate New York.

That day, she had realized that the ground she walked upon was a fluid, shifting thing, liable to heave beneath her and knock her down without a moment's warning. On that day, her old life had ended.

Suddenly Dylan loomed before her, holding out the cellular phone. "Here," he said softly. "Take it."

She stared at the phone—anything to avoid looking into his clear blue eyes. She was afraid that if she looked at him and saw kindness or understanding or pity, she would collapse into a quivering ball of tears. She simply could not find the words to explain. She wasn't sure she understood herself why all this was coming out here and now.

She took the phone into her hands.

"It must have been a terrible tragedy," he said, standing so close to her that she could feel his warmth, smell that man-scent of him, a strange mixture of sunlight and sweat. "He was a young man?"

Her words came out husky, dry. "He was twenty-eight when he died."

"You knew each other long?"

"We had been married for five years. Dating for five years before that."

"He stole you out of the cradle, then."

She managed a humorless twitch of a smile. "I was six-teen when we met. I felt quite old enough to choose a hus-band."

"I see."

She saw him making quick mental calculations. Deter-mining her age. He probably thought her much older than her thirty years. Most people did.

"I imagine," he continued, "that a number of lives were destroyed after that accident."

"Everyone on the plane died."

"Those weren't the lives I was talking about."

She glanced up and met his calm blue gaze. She tried to swallow the swell of emotion in her throat. "A year and a half in therapy. Yes, I'd say a few lives were destroyed."

"Casey, I'm—"

"Sorry. I know." She tightened her arms across her chest. "God, I learned to hate those words. Even though I know there's no other way to express sympathy. I just...I just heard them so much after Charlie died."

"Well, if it's any comfort, you've done well for yourself."

"Have I?" she asked, hefting the cellular phone aloft. "Have I, really?"

"Yes, you have," he insisted. "Look at the career you've built, the places you've gone—"

"And look how quickly I collapse into a ball of nerves," she interrupted, "as soon as I get into a situation where I have to depend on someone other than myself."

That was the crux of it, she realized. That was what was causing this fresh rush of pain through her, as if the membrane she'd stretched across the memories had burst. Here, lost in these woods with Dylan, she was in a situa-tion, for the first time in three long years, where she had to depend on another human being for her welfare.

She had vowed never to depend on someone else again.

She'd been clear about that soon after Charlie had died. She'd sold the house of her and Charlie's dreams, shipped the golden retriever to her sister in Connecticut and taken every penny of the settlement money with the airline to start this career of hers. To travel far, far away from the nucleus of her earlier life. Far away from her family. Her hometown. Her old job. She needed to keep traveling, keep moving, staying nowhere for more than three to six weeks, so that she would never again feel the ties that bound her to the rest of humanity. It hurt too much when they were ripped apart.

Then Jillian's voice came to her. Casey remembered all those little barbs—gentle barbs, for Jillian—about how not to confuse finding a new life with running from the old one.

In the dimming light of these deep woods, she suddenly saw herself clearly for the very first time.

"Casey?"

She glanced up at him. The rosy fingers of the sunset stretched through the trees and lit one side of his face. The world came into sharp focus; the screech of a jay in the leaves above, the rustle of a squirrel in the underbrush, the moist fecund scent of the quiet woods. Dylan's breathing, even and soft.

Something was changing. Something was changing inside her.

"Casey..." he began again, obviously struggling for words. "I know we don't know each other very well. Despite last night."

Color crept up her face. She bit her lip on the urge to tell him that he knew her better than any other living man.

"But," he continued, tapping the cellular phone in her hand, "I want you to pack this away for tonight."

A quiver of panic rippled through her anew. Her knuckles whitened around the phone. This was her backup. This was her way of protecting herself. She wasn't so sure she wanted to surrender her fate, even in this small way.

Where was Jillian now? Where were her rough-edged little comments about grief and recovery? Where were her barbed words that stuck in Casey's head whenever she faced a difficult situation? Somehow, she'd moved beyond Jillian's help. With a new clarity of thought, Casey realized that she'd taken the first real step out of therapy. And it all had something to do with this man standing in front of her.

"Casey..." He raked his hand through his hair. "I've worked for over a year to set up this trip. This is our first real setback. Give me a chance to work us out of it before we call in the cavalry."

"Dylan—"

"It's not so hopeless. I have a sense of where we are." He tapped his temple with a finger. "It's all up here, all the twists and turns of the day. I can get us back to the canoe. It's just going to take a little time. Give me twenty-four hours, and then you can do what you like."

She tightened her grip on the phone. She wondered if Dylan knew what he had just done. She wondered if he knew he was allowing her one step in the right direction, if she had the courage to take it. *One day at a time.* Twenty-four hours at a time. Jillian couldn't have thought up a better ploy.

She forced her mind to clear. She had to think straight. She took a deep, cleansing breath.

"Okay, Davy Crockett." She blinked her eyes open on the exhale. "You've got twenty-four hours."

DYLAN STRODE ALONG the dappled path. He caught sight of some moss growing on the north side of an oak and adjusted the direction of his steps accordingly. After a full day of wandering through these woods, he was convinced that if they continued trudging toward the southeast, they would eventually find the river they'd come from, and thus their abandoned canoe.

Casey plodded dutifully behind him. She'd spoken very little since she'd told him about her husband last night. She seemed lost in her own thoughts and reluctant to share those thoughts with him.

It had been a cold night in the tent, as well, and not just because of the unseasonable dip in the temperature. She'd slipped into the tent before him. When he'd entered, he had leaned down to run his fingers over her head. But she had given him such a soft, vulnerable look with those big brown eyes that he'd made himself back off. If the lady didn't want comforting, he wasn't going to force himself on her—even if he felt like crushing her in his arms and making all the hurt go away.

He couldn't imagine the hurt. But he was beginning to imagine what Casey Michaels was made of. He was beginning to realize that she'd been through the fires of hell and—despite her confidence and outward calm—she had not emerged unsinged.

He couldn't help something else, too. He'd spent a lot of time grappling with an odd sense of jealousy. Jealousy of a dead man. It would almost be worth dying, to know that a woman mourned you as deeply as Casey mourned her late husband.

He wanted to shake her free of ghosts and remind her how good it was to live. But, he thought, as he glanced up and noticed the lengthening of shadows across the ground, he wouldn't get much of a chance to be with her if he didn't find his way out of these woods soon.

He paused, catching a glimpse of a knotted old oak just to his right. He stopped in his tracks and peered through the trees.

Casey's footsteps slowed behind him. "Dylan?"

"Wait," he said. "I recognize something."

He broke through the brush and approached the old oak. He remembered this tree—older than the others around it, as if it had not been clear-cut whenever the rest of these woods had been, a hundred years or so ago. A distinctive knot bent the trunk at about eye level.

He scanned the surroundings, then caught sight of a sapling with a broken branch, and a narrow path beyond.

He set his foot upon the path. Casey must have sensed his excitement, because she, too, picked up her pace. The farther they traveled along the path, the more sure Dylan got.

A half-mile farther, as the sun cast the last of its golden light through the trees, he heard the gurgle of a river. He was carrying a hundred pounds on his back, but his feet felt light as he ran the last few yards. There, floating against the bank, was the canoe.

"Casey—look."

She crashed out of the woods behind him, pale, disheveled. An angry pink slash marked her leg where she'd been scratched by a branch in their wanderings. Yet as her gaze fell upon the canoe her face lit up with a smile worth a hundred thousand bucks.

She sank to the ground. The backpack landed first. She leaned back and used it as a pillow. She closed her eyes and stretched the back of her hand across her brow. She let her smile spread into a laugh—a nervous laugh that shimmered with relief.

He shrugged his backpack to the ground, walked to her side, then fell to his knees to unsnap the fasteners of her pack. He brushed off the straps and set her shoulders free, then worked on the buckle at her waist. Her face glowed with a sheen of perspiration, and tendrils of her hair clung to her temples, her neck. He brushed them out of the way and met the softness of her amber eyes.

"See," he said. "I told you we weren't lost."

Her smile lingered. Her chest rose and fell with the swiftness of her breath. "You're wrong," she whispered. "We *were* lost." She reached up and traced the edge of his brow. "But you found our way out."

He searched her eyes and saw, if not a lusty welcome, then at least not a plea to be left alone. So he did what he'd wanted to do since she'd told him of her sorrow. He took her face in his hands and kissed her.

She tasted of salt-sweat and heat. Her mouth moved softly beneath his. Her body flexed, arched. He felt her hands on his sides, clutching him harder, as the kiss deepened. He dragged the full length of his body atop hers and felt a rush of desire so strong and so fierce that he forced himself to pull away from her kiss.

"I missed you last night, Casey."

He wished he hadn't said the words. Damn his tongue. He was falling for this lady, too fast, too hard—and there was no reason why she had to know.

She wound an arm around his neck and raised her face to meet his. "Let's make up for lost time, then."

Her lips were hot, eager. He kissed her. Hard. Harder. He slipped an arm between her and her backpack, lifted her up, then yanked the pack out from under her. They rolled together on the ground until she lay on top of him. The grass felt cool and soft against his back. They were already damp with sweat, already hot from the exertion of hours of hiking through the woods, so he didn't know whether it was the situation or the fresh rush of desire coursing through his veins that caused the change—that caused a kiss at first hesitant and gentle to turn as fierce and frenzied as if they hadn't touched each other in weeks.

He bound her to him as tightly as he could, opened his mouth wider to taste her, so he could feel her cheek against his chin, his nose across her cheekbone, her hair brushing his brow. She made a sound deep in her throat—a wild little sound, enough to make him crazed.

He peeled her T-shirt off her body and tossed it away. He sank his teeth into the fleshy mound straining against the stretchy elastic of her bra. He slid his thumbs under the spandex of her running shorts and shoved them down, low enough so he could clutch the roundness of her bottom and force her hips against his loins.

She arched in that reckless, catlike way she had, forcing her tight little bottom up into his hands. He scraped his stubbly face across the thin elastic of her bra and found the peak of one nipple straining against the fibers and licked it. Again and again. Laving his tongue against her, feeling her whole breast tighten against his mouth. Then she tossed her head and made that little wild sound again.

He clutched her closer, shoved his hands lower, forced her legs to spread, found the moistness and heat of her with the tips of his fingers.

Then, suddenly, she pushed him away, clawed her fingernails over his abdomen, fumbled with the snap and zipper of his shorts. She plunged a hand under the band of his underwear and wrapped a grip around the center of his pleasure. And pulled. And pulled. Until he seized her arm, yanked it away from imminent danger and rolled her onto her back.

"No."

She spoke the word softly. With one surprisingly strong heave, she rolled him onto *his* back again and made short work of his shorts. He lay there, breathing more heavily than he had all day walking fifteen miles with a hundred pounds of weight strapped on his back, his need quite obvious. She stood, and with the setting sun casting her figure in shades of gold, she peeled off what was left of her clinging clothing while he watched.

Naked she fell upon him, swung a leg across his body, and made them one.

He squeezed his eyes shut and grasped her hips at the first tight thrust.

Ahh... She felt so good. She felt so right. They fit. As tight and close as two people could be. He curled his hand around her neck, and yanked her down so he could kiss her. So he could plunge his tongue into her mouth as he plunged another part of his body into another part of hers.

Later, not very much later, she cried out, and bells went off in his head. He told himself, very sternly, that these were definitely *not* wedding bells.

They lay for a long time upon the grass, their bodies glued together by sweat and the moisture of sex. He blindly traced the dappling of the last light of day upon her back, an excuse to hold her close. In the growing darkness, mosquitos rose from the shallow water, drawn to their heat.

Dylan reached for his pack without nudging her off him and yanked the bottle of mosquito repellent from a side pocket. With long, even strokes he covered her body.

She flinched and slapped the calf of her leg. From behind tangled hair she smiled at him and said, "You missed a spot."

"I missed a lot of spots," he murmured, running his hand across her breast. "And if we don't get into the tent soon, we're both going to have welts in very painful places."

They rose from their unlikely bed, slipped on their clothes, and went about the familiar ritual of setting up camp. They had not chosen the best campsite, trees blocked the evening breeze from sifting in to blow away the mosquitos. So, as soon as they'd driven in the last tent stake, they resigned themselves to a cold dinner, bombed the inside of the tent with repellent, and zipped themselves in.

He pulled out some shrink-wrapped hard cheese and salami and started cutting...but he didn't have much of an appetite.

He met her eyes across the glow of the lantern. "You realize," he said quietly, "that we didn't use a condom."

She lowered her gaze and nodded, once. "I know. Don't worry, the timing is all wrong."

"Timing?"

"I'm very regular," she explained. "I'm due in a few days. I thought we could take a chance...and that's about as much thought as I gave to it."

Then she lifted her gaze again, and he found himself caught in those hot brown eyes.

"I wasn't doing much thinking, either." He sank his Swiss Army knife into the salami. "But we'd best not take any more chances."

"Well...you know that we're running low, don't you?"

He knew she wasn't talking about food. "So we'll have to ration ourselves."

"We'll be okay for a few days, anyway."

He knew better than to play baby roulette. How many kids had he seen in his high school who took a chance "just once," and found themselves facing decisions hard enough for full-grown adults, never mind budding adolescents? And an urban school district sixty miles from Bridgewater had been struggling for over a year trying to decide whether to hand out condoms in the school. He was supposed to be a responsible adult. He was supposed to be a role model for the kids. Of course, the kids would never know about what had happened in the wilds of these woods.

Still, he was finding himself wondering if his and Casey's

baby would have the same soulful amber eyes as the woman sitting cross-legged in front of him.

God, he was a fool.

Before he said anything he would regret later, he decided the safest thing to do was to change the subject. He held out a slice of salami balanced on the blade of his knife. "Casey, tomorrow we're going to have to venture back into these woods, you know."

He saw the flash of fear. He saw, too, how quickly she hooded her eyes from his gaze.

"Yeah, well, I figured we wouldn't be staying here for the rest of the trip."

"You think you can handle it?" He sank his knife into the cheese. "You think you can trust me to find my way through this?"

She met his eyes then, gave him a searching gaze—wary, unsure. He met that gaze evenly.

Trust me, Casey. Trust me to get you out of here. Lean on my shoulder. I want your weight. I want your body. I want your trust. I want your...

He wanted too much. He always wanted too much. That was what drove them all away. He was getting the feeling that Casey would give him almost anything—her laughter, her courage, her body—rather than give him her trust.

Then she took a deep, deep breath. "I think I can handle it," she said in a soft voice. "For at least another twenty-four hours."

CASEY BURIED HER COPY of the map at the bottom of her backpack, along with the cellular phone. Jillian and all her twelve-step methods hadn't prepared Casey for this situation. But somehow, Casey sensed that it was the right thing to do.

In the two days that followed, as they tramped through

thick woods and canoed across narrow streams, she felt strangely disconnected. She knew she should be utterly terrified. They still hadn't found their way out of the woods. But since that evening on the banks of the river with Dylan, she felt as if she'd given something over to him. She suspected that something was called "trust."

So she'd followed him in silent detachment, touching his strong hand when he helped her across a ravine, holding his wide shoulders while they made love in the sunshine at lunchtime, listening to him discuss their next move, watching him peer, confounded, at the old map. She felt oddly buoyant. Light-footed. Calmhearted.

She knew this strange sense of peace might be nothing more than a defense mechanism. A way to disassociate from the true situation. Whatever it was, it was keeping her going. That was all she expected from herself.

Now, she gripped the worn handle of her paddle and twisted it according to Dylan's commands, as they searched the banks of yet another narrow stream for some sort of marker. She watched the familiar flex of that broad back and felt a tingle deep in her abdomen.

She had been right, that first night when they had made love. Dylan was a strong man, a good man. Whatever happened at the end of this adventure, she would leave it lighthearted. She would leave it a better person, a stronger person, for having known his touch.

Then she would drive to Connecticut, to her sister's house with her sister's fine husband and two lovely children, and maybe she wouldn't feel that familiar gripping sadness. For this time, she would have a story to tell that would ease her sister's worry. Casey had slept with a brawny man through three weeks of a camping adventure. Casey was no longer dead to the world.

"Casey?"

"Hmm?"

"If you don't start paying attention, you're going to rip a hole in the bottom of this canoe."

Casey glanced away from Dylan and realized the bow of the canoe was headed straight for the shore. "Oh!" She twisted the paddle and set them on a more even course.

"So..." He glanced over his shoulder. His blue eyes twinkled with mischief. "What were you thinking?"

"I was wondering when we were going to stop for lunch."

"It's only ten o'clock, Casey."

"I know."

"How would you like some fresh fish?"

"Fish?" She wasn't much of a fish lover. She preferred crustaceans—shrimp or lobster, drowning in butter—but right now she would eat just about anything that wasn't hard salami or dehydrated soup or freeze-dried beef stew. "You mean, real fish?"

"Yep." He gestured to a small cove just ahead. "I see a whole bunch of pike riding in those shallows. Should be a breeze to catch."

"You said you wanted to find that marking before sundown."

"Heck, we're already three days behind schedule. Another couple of hours won't matter."

She saw the twinkle in his eye, then twisted the paddle and headed them toward shore.

An hour later Casey crouched over the fire, gingerly poking two very tender fish filets around a saucepan, trying not to let her drool sizzle into the pan. The aroma of roasted fish filled the clearing. She found herself remembering the smell of her mother's house every year after her father came home from his salmon-fishing stints in the great

Northwest. For weeks they would eat salmon, and the smell would fill the house.

She'd always associated the odor with her father's return from his trip. A time of great joy, despite the horrid stench. She hadn't thought about that in years.

She wondered where Dylan had run off to. He'd caught the fish with surprising ease, then boned and filleted them for her. She'd promised to cook them while he went off to scout the terrain. At the time, she'd been too thrilled by the prospect of fresh meat to think about the fact that she was alone in the woods.

Now she heard the crackle of his footsteps coming along a narrow path by the riverbank. She jumped up to greet him.

"'Bout time you got back," she said. "Another few minutes, and I'd have eaten both of these myself."

Dylan looked up. He had a strange expression on his face. She took two steps toward him. "Dylan? What's wrong?"

He held out his hand. "Come, I want to show you something."

"The fish—"

"Take them off the fire and cover them. This will only take a minute." He glanced toward her pack. "And bring your camera, too."

She hardly had time to cover the pan, prop it on a level rock and dig out her camera before he'd headed back down the path. Her stomach growled, but she didn't complain. Something was up—and so was her curiosity.

He paused a quarter mile along the riverbank, where the greenery broke to show a triangular stretch of muddied shore. He waited for her to catch up.

"Look." He gestured to a vine-covered shape slanting at a strange angle near a tree. He picked away one of the vines to show a gleam of pottery. "Does this look familiar to you?"

She poked around the vines. It was a jug of some sort, half beige, half brown, with a small finger-grip near the narrow mouth. The jug had been braced, upside down, upon a sturdy piece of wood, now twisted with vines.

When she said nothing, Dylan reached in and shoved away some clinging vines. There, on the creamy face of the pottery, were the markings of a distinct crest. "Dylan, that's..." She glanced up at him. "Is that what I think it is?"

"My grandfather's marking." A strange, boyish smile crossed his face. He jerked his chin toward the path beyond the riverbank. "This must be the end of that portage we couldn't find before. This must be the marker for people coming from Canada." He shook his head. "This is one of my grandfather's jugs. He used it to mark the portage."

She held his gaze as the import of his words sank in. He'd found it. He'd found the path. They knew where they were now; they could follow the map for the rest of the way into Canada.

She should feel incredible relief, but that wasn't what filled her heart. For she knew that better than finding their way, was that Dylan had found proof—solid, undeniable proof—that his grandfather had been telling the truth.

"Well, Dylan," she said, letting a grin spread wide across her face. "Congratulations. You've just proved your grandfather was a bootlegger."

"I'll be damned, Casey," he said, shaking his head. "I had hoped I might find this. But I didn't really believe I would."

Her first reaction, standing there smiling into Dylan's suddenly pensive face, was that this would make excellent copy. With her journalist's eye she could see the photo already, perhaps gracing the cover of *American Backroads*.

She'd already started writing the copy in her head, focusing on the human-interest aspect.

But her more immediate, more overwhelming reaction was to hold Dylan in her arms. Shake him, until he let those tears of joy flow instead of suppressing them like a man.

Then she moved into his arms. He slipped his hands across her back and pressed his nose into her hair. She felt him swelling, under all those bulging muscles. A swell of pride. A swell of unexpressed emotion.

He disengaged himself a few moments later. She let him go. It was too much emotion—too deep, too strong. He flashed her a wide smile and struck a swaggering pose by the jug.

"Well," he said, "start shooting, Casey. The MacCabe clan isn't going to believe this unless I have hard photographic evidence."

BY THE TIME THEY returned to the campsite the fish was dry and lukewarm, but Casey ate it as if it had been served to her on china at a fine restaurant. They'd found some ripe blackberries as well, and now she crusted the fruit over the last of the melba toast and savored its tart sweetness.

Dylan sat hunkered over the map, a baseball cap shading his eyes from the midday sun.

"We're farther up than I thought we were," he said. "It won't be long now."

"That's good," she mumbled around a mouthful of berries and cracker. "We were due today or tomorrow, so maybe they won't send out the National Guard if we're home soon." She paused as a thought came to her. "How soon?"

"Three days. Maybe two."

She paused in her chewing. "Is that all, Dylan?"

"Mm-hmm."

She held the cracker in her fingers. Her gaze drifted across the glittering gurgle of the river. The campfire smoke curled blue into the canopy of leaves above. A fish jumped, snatching a dragonfly from the surface of the water. A cardinal swooped through the trees on the other side of the river, a flash of red in the deep green shadows.

She took a bite and chewed, slowly. Two or three more days of camping. She should be ecstatic. In two or three days she could stop taking baths in river water. She could actually use a real toilet. She could drink a whole gallon of freshly squeezed orange juice. She could sink her teeth into an apple.

Two or three more nights in the quiet of the woods, alone with this man. Two or three more nights of lovemaking.

Dylan's face was shielded by the bill of the baseball cap. She couldn't tell what he was thinking. She wasn't even sure what she was thinking—or feeling.

She leaned over and peered at the map. "Is that where we are?" She pointed at a red X on the map, and Dylan nodded. "But look at the distance we have to cover." She traced the twist of the trail over the border. "That can't possibly be two or three days—it's too far."

"We'll be covering it really quickly."

"Oh yeah?" She sank back on her haunches and popped the last of the cracker into her mouth. "Do I look like a marathon runner?"

"Yes." He glanced up at her from under the bill of the baseball cap and gave her legs a long, hot look-over. "But we'd be covering it quickly nonetheless."

"Dylan..."

"Casey, remember before we started this journey, when I mentioned something about white water...?"

10

"CASEY, WATCH *RIGHT!*"

Casey braced her feet on the ribs of the canoe just as the river dropped. She twisted the paddle with a jerk. The bow of the canoe crashed into the foam. A boulder shot by them, pounded by the current. The cold spray blinded her. She sputtered and shook her hair out of her face. On white water, Dylan had told her, she couldn't be blind for a second.

"Casey, watch *left. Left!*"

She fought with the current for control of her paddle. She flexed her fingers over the smooth wood and yanked. The canoe jerked, swerved, skidded sideways on the river and shot spray over the gunwale. Through the mist she caught a glimpse of the corpse of a fallen tree jutting into the stream, just as they skimmed by it.

Dylan knelt in the bow, bobbing like a skier lurching from mogul to mogul. His paddle lay flat across the canoe, his hands braced on it and the gunwales, his thighs taut and spread as he leaned forward, surveying the misty trail for eddies and haystacks and all the other colorfully-named sources of danger in white water. Spray soaked him, darkened his hair, sent rivulets careening down his thighs.

This was the picture she wanted for *American Backroads.* This picture, of him and her, working together on this wild, raging river, breathing the same air, thinking the same thoughts, working like one creature. She kept her eyes on the back of his head, straining to hear his commands above the roar of the water. They'd only ridden these ragged streams for two days, but they'd covered twice the distance as when they'd been canoeing against the current. And they'd found a wild rhythm together. To go with the one they shared every spare moment they could find.

She flexed her hands over the paddle. There was a strange exhilaration in riding this white water. She and Dylan had eaten away a lot of the baggage over the past weeks, so the lightened canoe rode buoyantly on the waves. Maybe the weeks of experience helped, too, for now as she made her paddle act as a rudder, she felt like she really controlled the canoe far more than during all those days of plodding upstream. Even though the current roared against the birchbark beneath her feet. Even though the white water battered the sides. Even though jagged rocks threatened just under the surface of the river, tracing paths in the dried black pitch that streaked the canoe.

"Left, Casey! *Watch left!*"

She plunged the paddle deeper, twisted the shaft, felt the canoe lurch to her command. Spray bit into her thighs and iced her feet. The canoe heaved, rose in the river, then touched back down into the foam.

"Curve coming up!" he shouted over his shoulder. "Easy, girl. Take it loose."

Dylan plunged his paddle into the spray, breaking the hurl of their trajectory as much as he could. Casey glimpsed the curl of the river ahead, walled on one side by sheer granite. Dylan shouted instructions. With care they edged out of the central trough into a deep-water eddy.

He paddled them into the shadows, into the lee of a boulder. The canoe twisted in the weak whirlpool. From this vantage point, they could see the drop in the river ahead of them, and the rise of mist in the trees.

He gestured down river, toward the billow of the mist. "We'd better take a look at that before we run it."

"Why? You told me none of these rapids would be worse than Class II."

"Yeah, but I didn't expect the water level to be so low. That could change things."

"C'mon, Dylan," she teased, "where's your sense of adventure?"

Dylan cast her a white-toothed grin. "Is this the woman whose face turned ashen when I mentioned white water?"

"Hey, I was thinking of the Snake River, not this little creek."

"So, think you can take more?"

"Oh, yeah," she said, slicking her hair off her face. She knew she was grinning wildly—as wildly as he was. She knew, too, that he was loving this as much as she was.

That thought should have scared her. She'd not been this close to a man since Charlie. She'd not been this close to anybody since Charlie's death. She'd not wanted to know the intricate messages that a man could give a woman, by the slightest tilt of his head, by the intensity of his gaze, by the way he leaned forward.

Yet here they were, as close as a man and a woman could get, alone in the wilds, racing headlong toward civilization. And she felt happy. *Happy.*

She told herself to stop analyzing it and just enjoy.

He made no move to turn the bow back into the current. He was simply staring at her. "Did anyone tell you you look good when you're wet?"

"Yes," she said, as a frisson skittered down her spine. "You."

"Sure you don't want to take a nice long walk along the river before we run these rapids...?"

For a response, Casey plunged her paddle into the water and headed toward the shore.

There they found a patch of soft moss bathed in golden sunlight. There, Casey peeled off her wet clothes in the open air, while Dylan did the same. There, she let him wrap his muscled arms around her body and pull her to the ground.... There, in the bright August sunshine, he dipped his head between her legs and did wondrous things with his lips and teeth and tongue until she was blinded by much more than the sunshine.

Much later, both of them laughing and sated, Casey shrugged into one of Dylan's dry T-shirts and her damp shorts and strapped on a light backpack. They headed down the riverbank to scout the terrain. Dylan interlaced his fingers with hers as they walked; their hands joined felt like the most natural thing in the world.

A way down the riverbank they stumbled upon a small clearing. The cold charcoal remains of a bonfire blackened the center of it, and brown and green beer bottles littered the ground.

Dylan shook his head and started collecting the debris.

Casey joined him. "Guess they never heard of 'Take only pictures, leave only footprints.'"

"Probably a bunch of teenagers partying."

"Hmm."

"We can't be far from civilization now."

Not far from civilization now. Casey tipped a beer bottle to drain the rainwater out of it, then turned away so Dylan couldn't see her face. They'd talked about being close to the end of their voyage, but this was the first time she'd been faced with physical evidence.

They had so little time. So little time.

For, surely, their relationship wouldn't last beyond this trip. How could it? What else could she do but climb back into Bessie and set off for her sister's place and another assignment? The only plan she had beyond that was to give Jillian a call and tell her the whole wonderful story...and let her know that she wouldn't be calling anymore—at least not for therapy. Then, Casey supposed, she would set off down the road again with a mended spirit.

Odd. That the world seemed so alien. Three weeks in the woods and suddenly she felt like she'd shed another life.

She cast Dylan a sidelong glance. She wondered what he would do at the end of this voyage. Would he touch her cheek and say goodbye and not look back? Or would he ask her to stay?

For all their intimacy, they'd never talked about it. The truth was that she didn't even know how he felt about her. She didn't know if he considered her just another woman in his life, or if he was expecting something more once they finished their project here together. They never talked about it.

She told herself it didn't matter. Whatever happened between them, she would be forever grateful to Dylan for chipping her out of the ice block she'd been living in, for teaching her how to trust again.

Suddenly he was standing beside her, taking an upended bottle from her hand. "I think that's the last of them, Casey. We'll pack them in along with all the other garbage."

"You're such a good Boy Scout."

He didn't move away. She glanced up into his eyes. Hooded eyes. Wary. Careful. "You know, Casey...I think we can do this."

She looked at him blankly, not quite sure what he was saying.

"This part of the river," he added, in answer to her unspoken question. "I think we can run it."

"Oh."

"But it's not going to be easy," he continued. He lifted his shoulders in a strange little shrug. "A trip like this is never easy. And the hardest part always seems to be at the end."

He was standing close, very close. She smelled the river on him, saw the flecks of stubble on his cheek, remembered with vivid, knee-melting intensity the feel of his beard scraping her inner thigh.

"I know what I'm talking about," he explained. "I've made a lot of these trips. Too many. And for all the wrong reasons. But the end is the tricky part."

She wondered what he was jabbering about, and wished he wouldn't stand so very close. "Well, if you think we can do it..."

"I'd like to try." He slipped his hand into hers. "There're going to be a few rough patches. We'll have to take a couple of quick turns, maybe back up a bit before we can go forward. But if you really want to do this," he said, leaning close to her, "then I'm game."

She felt his breath upon her face. He was looking deeply into her eyes. And she suddenly realized he was talking about more than the river rapids.

Though she stood on solid ground, she felt, suddenly, as if she'd shifted into the river, as if the current had swept her legs out from under her and pushed her into places unknown, uncharted worlds; into cold water that was quite over her head—and she with no paddle.

She held tightly to his hand and pressed her face against his. She breathed in the scent of him, woodsy and clean. He moved his face against hers, sought her lips and found them.

It was a sweet kiss. Soft and loving. She stepped closer, pressed her body against his, for this she understood: the wanting, the yearning, the passion. But Dylan ran his hands up her arms and gripped her shoulders and eased her head down into the nook between his jaw and his shoulder.

He held her. Just held her. She heard his heart thumping slowly and evenly in his chest.

"Well, Casey," he murmured. "What do you think? Are we going to run this river or not?"

She closed her eyes and listened to his heart. She let the warmth of him seep into her skin. She let herself feel the strength of his arms around her, the breadth of his strong shoulders. Then she took a deep breath.

"All right," she whispered on the exhale. "Let's give it a try."

CASEY KNEW SHE WAS in trouble at the first drop of the river.

These rapids weren't like the others. These rapids *raged*. They seized the canoe and hurled it downstream and all but mocked her efforts at control. Dylan barked out commands and she struggled to hold the paddle still, but the canoe seemed to skim across the water like a car on ice, catching pavement now and again but soon spinning wildly across the surface.

They lurched past boulders at blinding speed; careened against the current, then slipped nose-first into it again. Twice she was lifted completely off her seat by the heave of the vessel, twice more her bottom slapped back onto the splintered board. She felt the jerk of the first impact, heard the screech of rock through the belly of the vessel, and saw the bubble of water surge through the finger-long rent in the canoe, but had no time to stanch it or even to head toward shore, for the current gripped the boat and shot it recklessly down the central trough and she had her hands full just trying to fight for control.

A thought fluttered through her mind— *We've got a rip. It'll take a full day to fix it.*

"Right."

Dylan's voice rang out in the vapor curling around them.

"Right," he repeated. *"Right!"*

She yanked with all her weight and the canoe bucked, then swerved, and another nest of debris flew by them.

"Left, Casey—"

She surged the other way, twisted the paddle, felt a splinter sink deep into her palm.

"Pull it, pull it, Casey—"

Dylan plunged his paddle into the river, sending up a fountain of spray. The canoe heeled, sidled, slowed, edged off the trough of the current. Casey felt the water cover her shoes, inch up her ankles.

"We got a rip. Gotta get this thing out of here!" he shouted. "Keep her on the edge of the current—less pull."

Sweat broke out on her forehead, only to be washed away by spray as they careened past a submerged boulder. Dylan plunged his paddle into the river like a spear into a fish, holding tight with two hands while kneeling up, as high as he dared, looking forward for safety.

They rode the edge of the current, and it was like being on the lip of a water slide—a tenuous balancing act. Dylan had been right, the water level was low, and so they rode not too far above the rocky bottom of the river, with its jagged array of granite chips. The only indication of any danger below the surface was a suspicious spray or a knot in the current, not easy to see with the mist the river spewed up all around them, but Dylan seemed to sense where they were and eased them around the dangers.

Still, even out of the center trough, they shot downstream far too fast. Casey quivered on the edge of control. She thought she might be terrified, but she didn't have a heck of a lot of time to think about it. Nor any time to take deep cleansing breaths. For they were falling, falling, down a slick chute with no eddies to veer into for safety, and no good open place along the riverbank to rest. She felt, oddly, as if she were playing a video game, but her joystick wasn't working right.

The shock of the cold water on her face was enough to remind her this wasn't a video game. That and the tenseness of Dylan's muscles as he crouched in the bow, jerking his paddle to one side, then another, all senses alert for reprieve.

Then, suddenly, he said, "Uh-oh."

It was a small sound, but to her it sounded like a shout. "Dylan?"

"Trouble coming."

"Trouble coming? Trouble *coming*? I'm up to my ankles in the river and you're telling me—"

"Hard right, Casey, then a sharp left."

"Hard right? But we'll get sucked up into—"

"Better than getting splintered."

"Dylan—"

"Hard right. *Now!*"

She reacted by instinct. She lunged toward the left, twisting her paddle flat against the current. The canoe bucked and slid as smooth as ice into the torrent of the river.

"Left. *Left!*"

She surged the other way, rotating the paddle. The wood strained under the assault. The canoe veered, centered, then veered again, and she heard the scrape of rock against wood as they barreled past another obstacle.

She saw a flap of bark hanging off the side and said, "We've got another rip."

Dylan glanced over his shoulder for a second and eyed the flap of bark hanging off the gunwale. "Surface. High up on the canoe. We'll be okay."

"The water's rising, Dylan."

"We're almost done."

"Are we having fun yet?"

She heard his laugh, high above the water, reckless and wild, a delirious, infectious sort of laugh. She felt it bubble up inside her, too, despite the danger—maybe because of the danger. Yes, maybe because of the danger.

And for the first time in her life Casey could understand all the daredevils she'd ever interviewed. It came to her with a sudden crystal clarity; they did it for moments like this. For the utter quivering exciting thrill. For the rush of adrenaline and flood of excitement—for the thrill of living on the edge of life itself.

She *was* having fun. She was having more fun than she'd ever had in her life. In this flash of a moment, riding these waves with Dylan in the bow, she felt more alive than she'd ever felt before. She was brightly, sharply, tinglingly alive.

This is why I love this man.

It was that simple. She loved him for taking her to the edge she'd been afraid to approach. She loved him for teaching her how to risk again. She realized she'd spent three years of her life away from everyone she loved, afraid that death would pluck someone else from her life and leave her mourning. She'd spent three years interviewing men and women who had no fear of looking death in the face—because she couldn't.

Dylan had given her back her life.

"Dylan?" She cried out his name, but the wind of their passage plucked the words from the air. Then Dylan shouted something. His words fragmented against the breeze, against the solid granite wall of the cliff to their right.

"What? Dylan, I can't—"

He jerked to face her. "Left, Casey, *left!*"

They slammed into something. Casey heard a sound like

a gunshot, then realized, in the split second before she tumbled out of her seat and sprawled headlong over the gear,
that the gunwale of the canoe had snapped. She heard Dylan grunt, then saw him tumble back. The sky whirled
above her and then the canoe heaved up and capsized,
dumping everything into the drink.

She sucked in a breath before the river yanked her under.
The current seized her legs first and dragged her down so
fast it forced her arms up. She shot down the torrent on her
belly like a human luge. She couldn't scream. Her ears
ached at the suck of the icy water past them. Everything
was white and roaring and her knees scraped the rocky
bottom. She struggled to lift her head up above the surface
but there didn't seem to be a surface, just a world of spray
and bubbles. The life jacket was useless, it got sucked down
as easily as she had. She kicked and scratched, trying to
find a foothold, then, just as suddenly as she'd been pulled
under, she was spit up and thrown bodily against an obstacle.

She gasped for air and grasped blindly for a handhold.
She pressed her cheek against a rough surface and realized
it was a log jutting into the river. She hefted herself up to
her chest. Amid the roar she knew only one truth: She had
to get out of the water.

Somehow, she pulled and yanked and clawed herself to
the riverbank without dislodging the fallen tree. The riverbank was steep and uneven. She slipped twice. She felt
something sharp bite into her knee. She clambered up,
gripping the roots of saplings and handfuls of moss, until
she'd squeezed herself up and out of danger.

She closed her eyes and laid her cheek on a bed of moss.
She was trembling uncontrollably. She knew she was in
shock. Sensations came to her strangely disconnected. A
warm rivulet of blood dripped down her shin. Her palms

smarted as if the river bottom had shaved off two layers of skin. Her side ached, where she'd slammed against the tree trunk.

"Dylan?"

Her voice came out low, hoarse, shaky. She licked her lips and swallowed, then raised her head and forced her voice louder.

"Dylan?"

She couldn't panic. She needed to find help. She needed to find Dylan. She winced as she pushed herself to a sitting position to scan the river. No Dylan in sight. No gear in sight. No canoe in sight.

She scrambled to her feet, ignoring the shot of pain up her side. *Think. Think.* She had no idea how far she'd traveled downstream. She had no idea whether Dylan was caught farther upstream, or whether he'd been swept on down.

She headed upstream first. She squeezed through the thick woods, rushing through the brush, peering as far as she could see through the dense growth. She caught sight of some debris caught on a bush overhanging the river—it looked like clothing. She couldn't get close enough to tell whose it was.

She stopped and started walking in a tight little circle. *Dylan. Dylan.* She had visions in her head of Dylan's broken body caught against a boulder; Dylan's shirt caught in a bush and his head underwater; Dylan unconscious, slammed against boulders. She had visions of farmland strewn with twisted metal and bits of clothing and seat cushions hanging from trees.

She caught her lip on the quiver of a sob. *No.* No, she couldn't panic. Not now. She called his name. Heedless of the thickness of the woods, the close fit of sapling against sapling fighting for space, she surged downstream.

Branches whipped her face, tore at her clothes. She couldn't panic, not now.

She started to run. She knew her knees hurt with every jar, but it was a faraway sort of sensation, for her world was peeling into two. She recognized this sensation; she'd lived it before. It was as if she were hanging back, hovering over herself, watching herself make decisions and go through the motions of searching for Dylan; and this part of her hovering high in the trees was the calm part, the detached part, the quiet part—the safe part.

She saw herself scan the river. She saw herself recognize a backpack bobbing on the current, rising from deep under the water and then shooting up out of it. A tear rent its side and the contents tumbled out with each twirl out of the river, as if it were some sort of predator's prey being disemboweled, then consumed.

But there was no Dylan attached to it.

From a faraway place she heard herself shout. She saw herself hurl through the woods. She saw herself scrape her battered hands on the rough bark of birch trees, and trip on upraised roots. A clock ticked in her mind— *How long can a man last underwater? The cold will help, yes.* Yes, the cold would help. She'd once taken a CPR class at the community college after her grandfather had had a stroke and had come to live with her parents. How many seconds was she supposed to wait between breaths? She couldn't remember. She just couldn't remember—

"Dylan!"

The tightness in her chest— Yes, she remembered this. She remembered this pain.

"Dylan!"

11

DYLAN HEARD CASEY'S voice long before he heard her crashing through the woods. He stopped in his tracks and gripped a sapling so he wouldn't fall to his knees in relief.

"Casey! Over here!"

She made a strange sound, a half shout, half cry. He saw a flash of her between the trees. *She's all right. Oh, God, she's all right.* When he'd gone under he'd caught a glimpse of her sliding down the river, but that was the last he saw before he, too, had been sucked under. Then he'd rolled around in the surf, scoured against the granite wall, and done the best he could to struggle to safety.

He straightened as he saw her, wincing as pain shot through him. He hadn't taken a moment to catalog his own injuries once he'd scrambled out of the river. He was too worried about Casey. Now, he realized he might have broken a rib or two. He couldn't tell; he was too cold, and he was more concerned about the woman struggling out of the thicket toward him.

By the way she was moving, all her limbs seemed to be intact. Blood coursed down both her knees and stained the dirty canvas of her sneakers. Her face was as white as snow under the red welts that crossed her cheeks. She froze to the spot when she caught sight of him. Her eyes were wide and strangely wild.

All he could think as he stumbled toward her was *Thank God, thank God, thank God, thank God, thank God....*

He should never have asked her to run these rapids. If the water level had been higher, they would have been safe. But this late in the summer the water was low and fast and splintered by debris. She'd gotten so good at it. He'd been too eager to see her smiling wide with her eyes full of excitement, he'd been too eager to encourage the daredevil he now knew lived within her.

But there was more to it. He'd wanted her to depend on him. He'd wanted her to put her wholehearted trust in him. He'd wanted to look in her eyes when she made that decision. Because if he could get Casey to trust him, maybe, just maybe, he could also get her to love him. For Dylan had come to the inescapable conclusion that he'd fallen in love—all over again.

Damn him for being a fool, he thought, as he made his way toward her, wincing with every step. But if he didn't feel like he'd been kicked by a horse, he would fall to his knees and asked the woman to marry him right here, right now.

Something made him pause as he reached her. She just stood there. Shivering. Breathing hard. Staring at him with those strange, wild eyes while water dripped down her face.

"Casey…are you all right?"

Her jaw tightened. One eyelid twitched. A shudder shook her body from head to foot. She managed a single croaky word.

"No."

Oh, God. He reached for her. "Is anything broken? Did you knock your head—"

She slapped his hand away. "No."

"What? What?" Then he saw the wide amber gaze she cast toward him, he saw the fear in those eyes, and part of his heart melted. "Aw, Casey…"

He lifted his arms to hold her, to pull her to his chest—but she lashed out and shoved his arms away.

In the second before she lunged at him, he saw a flash of indescribable rage in her eyes, and he caught a glimpse of a kind of pain he could not begin to imagine. Then, before he could see anymore, she lowered her head, raised her fists and pummeled his chest.

While he gritted his teeth against the pain shooting up his side, he tried to seize her by the wrists. She was fast, she was angry, and her knuckles were like eight little hammers on the bruised muscles of his chest and abdomen. He had to stop her from hurting him, but he didn't want to stop her from feeling her own pain. He had guessed that she'd been suppressing this pain for too many years. He wanted her to feel it and get over it, so she could get on with her life. A life with him, if he had his way.

So he bit the inside of his cheek as he let her vent her rage on his chest, guarding his weaker side as best as he could. Her wild dark hair swung around her head, spraying the woods with water. He sensed the moment when her cries turned to sobs and her punches weakened. It seemed to take a long time; it seemed he stood forever under these leafy trees while she struggled with her own demons. In the end she sagged, and he opened his arms to her.

But the fight was not quite over. She pushed away and stumbled back against a tree trunk. "No," she said, swiping her tears with the butt of a dirty hand. "No, no, no. Don't do that again, Dylan."

He stood with his arms spread out and tried to give her a smile. "What? Hold you? Or let you beat me bloody?"

He regretted the attempt at humor immediately. He let his smile die. By the sight of her tearstained face, this wasn't going to be as easy as he'd hoped for.

"You told me," she said in a voice hoarse with screaming and tears, "that we could do this."

"I thought we could."

"You were *wrong*."

She screamed the word, leaning forward as she did so, launching the sound through the woods with all the anger in her heart. Then, just as quickly, she leaned back against the tree trunk and hid her mouth with a trembling hand.

"No, Casey," he said softly, tenderly probing his bad side, "I wasn't wrong. We're here, aren't we? We're alive—"

"But for the grace of God—"

"Yeah, but we're *alive*."

"I *trusted* you!"

"Did I let you down?"

"*Yes*."

That, too, a shout, echoing on the granite walls beyond the river. "Casey, do you think for one minute, I'd have intentionally dumped us both into that river?"

Her brow furrowed, she shook her head, but she seemed incapable of speech.

"Of course not," he answered for her. "I want a shower, but I want a hot one. And I like my skin." He managed a tentative step in her direction. "We can't control everything that happens. And you can't spend a lifetime trying to be safe and comfortable, or you'll lead a dull life."

"Rather a dull life," she persisted. "We never should have done this. You could have been killed—"

"Yes, and so could you," he interrupted. "But we weren't, and the expedition will go on."

"Just like that," she whispered, and it was as if the effort took all her energy. "Just like that," she repeated. "You fall into mountain water and are pushed a mile or so over gravel until you don't have any skin left on your knees or hands and all you have to say is, 'The expedition will go on'?"

Her voice had risen with each word.

"I didn't lure you out here on the premise that there would be no risk. There is always risk, Casey. In everything we do."

"Stop it! You sound like Jillian."

"Who the hell is Jillian?"

"A friend. Someone I need to talk to, right now."

"Talk to me," he said, feeling his own anger burn. "Talk to *me*, Casey. I'm here, and I'm all ears. Or is it that you don't consider me a friend?"

Her gaze skittered away, nervous and fearful. "You can't help me— You don't understand."

"I'm the only one who can help you. I'm the only one who understands what just happened here on this river."

"That's not what I'm talking about."

"Isn't it? Isn't this all about choices, Casey? What choices we're about to make?" He swiveled and gestured toward the river. "We've been dumped in the river, we've lost our gear, we're miles from civilization and both of us are hurt and bleeding. What choice do we have? Should we sit here and mourn about the disaster? Should we hide our heads in the dirt? Should we run in another direction? Or should we pick up where we left off and keep going?"

"Is that what you did," she asked in a small, angry voice, "after your wives left? Just picked up where you left off and kept going?"

Then he turned and glared at her, for there was something accusing in her voice, something bitter and biting. And he began to wonder what all this hysteria, what all this anger, was really about.

"Yes, that's what I did," he retorted. "I picked up where I'd left off and kept going. And if you think that's the easier path, then think twice, lady, how easy it is walking around your own hometown wearing a pair of horns.''

Dylan jerked away and raked a hand through his hair. What the hell was going on here? What the hell were they talking about? All he wanted to do was crush her in his arms, but she looked as if she would shatter if he took another step too close. Instead they were standing here bleeding and yelling at each other, and it was as if the battering of the accident had ripped open more than flesh. For both of them.

Softly she asked, ''Why didn't you leave? Why did you stay?''

Dylan glared at her. He didn't want to talk about this. He was battered and beaten enough—he saw no reason to probe the wound. But she was calm for a moment. Quiet. Attentive. He supposed that alone was enough reason to talk about the unspeakable.

''I wasn't about to leave behind my family and friends.''

Yeah, it hurt. It hurt to know that he'd tried to have a family life twice—and failed twice. Miserably and publicly. It hurt even more to think about trying again.

Then he took a long look at Casey. *Casey.* With her sweet amber eyes a man could lose his soul in. He thought of her courage. Her sense of humor. Her passion. He thought of all those broken dreams she'd left behind—dreams he would like to mend for her, and for him. He thought of the child they could have together, a babe with her eyes and her hair. And he told himself, for the hundredth time, that it would be worth it.

''Wife number one stole my pride,'' he said, ''but I wasn't about to let her steal everything else I valued. And wife number two was a mistake from the start.'' He held her gaze. ''But I got a taste of what happiness could be in each of those marriages. I want that. I've always wanted it. I'd given up on it...until now."

Her eyes widened. She pressed back against the tree. She turned her face away and thrust her fingers through her hair. She looked worn, pinched with exhaustion, and she wasn't meeting his gaze. He sensed he was pushing her too hard, talking too close to his heart, and scaring the hell out of her.

So he swallowed the proposal rising in his throat. So he swallowed impatience. They had time, they had time. It would take days for them to gather their equipment. They might have to walk the remaining miles to the St. Lawrence River. He had time. Best not to bare his heart to a woman on the verge of hysteria.

So, instead, he mustered a smile. "Now, Casey," he said, clutching his aching side, "do you want to tell me why we're talking about my ex-wives while we're both freezing, bleeding and soaking wet?"

She stilled and looked up at him.

"C'mon." He curled his fingers around her arm, and tugged her, gently, downstream. "Let's see what we can salvage of our gear, and then I'll bind up those knees of yours."

"Allô!"

At the sound of the voice, Dylan straightened too fast; he winced and stiffened as pain shot through his side.

"Dylan?" Casey tossed a pair of dripping-wet shorts across a low-lying branch, then limped to his side to peer through the trees. "Did you hear somebody?"

He spoke through gritted teeth. "Yeah, I think—"

"Allô!"

Casey gasped, then she sprang into action. "Over here!"

She crashed past a branch fluttering with wet laundry. "Here we are! Over here!"

"Ah! *Mam'selle*," came the voice. "*Je viens*— I'm coming!"

With Casey out of sight, Dylan took the opportunity to wince. His side throbbed painfully. He had not wanted to alarm Casey, but he really did think he'd broken a rib. He'd almost passed out when he'd pulled the remains of the canoe off the debris that had caught it. One look at the ripped and tattered craft had been enough to tell him that they would be walking the last miles to the St. Lawrence River. With her battered, swelling knees and his aching side, the smart thing to do was send up flares or, better yet, use that cell phone of hers—if they could ever find it.

Still, he'd wanted to see if he could tough it out. He'd wanted to finish this voyage under his own steam. She knew they were close. But most of all, he'd wanted to stay here, in the solitude of these woods, until he could get Casey to look him in the eye again. She'd been squirrelly and jumpy for the past hour, and he'd wanted her warm and pliant at his side.

But now, by the sound of her babbling and the laughing response of a distinctly French-Canadian voice, it looked as though they were saved.

He straightened, inch by inch, as they came closer, and composed his face as best he could.

"Dylan, look—the cavalry."

Casey limped into the small clearing with a dark-haired ranger in tow. The man nodded his head toward Dylan and held out a hand.

"Pierre Lefèbvre, Canadian Forestry Service," he said, his words lilting with a Québecois accent. "I have met Mam'selle Michaels. You must be MacCabe."

"Dylan." He gripped the man's hand. "It's good to see another face."

"*Oui*," he said, glancing around at the debris. "I see that."

"How did you find us?"

"Oh," he said, shrugging, "it was easy." He pulled a pile of frothy wet cloth from under his arm. "I followed a very pretty trail."

He shook out the material until Casey saw, among the clothes, her high-cut cotton underpants. Her face brightened and she snatched the lingerie from his hands. "Saved by my underwear," she muttered. "There's a first."

"I should inform you that this is littering," the man said, his dark eyes bright and teasing on Casey. "Big fines. Jail time in certain parts of Quebec—"

"Yeah," Dylan remarked, a jealous edge in his voice. "But you crossed the river. You're out of your jurisdiction."

"Seems so." He sighed and gave another Gallic shrug. "It was all in the interests of international cooperation."

"International…"

"The two of you have many people worried," the ranger explained. "There are twenty Yankees in a hotel just over the border. They've called everyone but your American FBI to find you."

Dylan rolled his eyes. His family must have been driving the Canadians crazy. "We're a few days late."

"*Oui*, so I've been told," Pierre said. "And so, here I am, the search party." His gaze drifted over the clothes and debris lying all around the clearing and settled on the battered canoe. "Bad accident, eh?"

"We lost most of our gear."

"There's a logging road a mile west of here. I've got a Jeep." His gaze flickered over Dylan, then Casey, and lingered on her bloodied knees. "Let me drive you into Canada. There's a hospital just over the border."

"Yes," Casey said on a sigh. "Yes, that would be wonderful."

Dylan glanced at her sharply. He wanted to do this on his own. He wanted to arrive on the banks of the St. Lawrence on his own steam, even if it meant walking across craggy ground for the last few miles. But Casey looked pale, tired, edgy. He knew he couldn't push her any farther, even if he planned to push himself beyond endurance.

"You two go," he said. "Take most of the gear. But I'm going to finish this."

"Dylan—"

"I made a promise to myself that I'd see the St. Lawrence when this was all through, Casey, come hell or high water."

"Go ahead," said the ranger, giving his Gallic shrug. "We will wait for you."

Dylan stilled, while the ranger's dark eyes sparkled.

"The banks of St. Lawrence," the ranger added, "lie a quarter mile to the north, just over that rise."

CASEY RESTED HER HEAD against the seat in the back of the Jeep, grateful for Pierre's unceasing chatter. He kept talking, even though she and Dylan were answering him in polite monosyllables. The Jeep lumbered and lurched over the old logging road, but Casey didn't even mind the battering. She was so relieved that they were heading for civilization. She was so relieved that this whole trip was over.

Her knees ached. Her hands stung. Her head throbbed. She felt nauseous. Ever since the accident she'd felt as if the whole world was spinning around her. She needed to get away from Dylan. She needed to get away from herself. She needed to think.

She soon became aware that they'd reached paved

ground. She opened her eyes long enough to see the steel rails of a bridge flying by, and below, the slate blue waters of a very wide river.

"The St. Lawrence," Dylan said, to no one in particular. "I saw it from that spit of land, sticking out from the southern shore. It was more impressive up close."

At the other end of the bridge a guard waved them to a stop, but after a rapid conversation with Pierre in French, the guard rolled his eyes, laughed, and waved them through.

Pierre drove them straight to a small hospital on the edge of the border town. He told her the lyrical name of the village, but it flew right out of her head. She was beginning to realize that she was in shock, for the memories of the past few hours were splintering right before her eyes—even as the pain in her knees and head intensified.

In the quiet emergency room they said goodbye to Pierre, who promised to drive straight to the hotel to drop off what they'd retrieved of their gear and inform the MacCabes where he'd left them. Then the nurses took her and Dylan to separate rooms for examination.

She needed a few stitches in both her knees. A pretty dark-eyed nurse clucked her tongue as she bathed the scratches that riddled Casey's face and legs. Casey found out that they'd taken Dylan up to radiology for X rays.

"X rays!" Casey exclaimed. "For what? Where?"

"His chest," the nurse said. "They think he might have broken a couple of ribs."

Lord, Casey thought. *And he hadn't said a word.* And he'd stubbornly walked that last quarter mile to the banks of the St. Lawrence River and back. While she'd babbled and complained and done everything but have a nervous breakdown.

An hour later, Casey limped out to the waiting room to find Dylan waiting for her. He lumbered to his feet to greet her. She tried to stifle the strange flicker of panic she felt at the sight of him, all tanned and golden-haired and steady eyed. Somehow he looked different amid the bright white walls of the hospital. Bigger. Gruffer. More dangerous.

She let her gaze drop to his T-shirt, where she could see the padding of a bandage. "They told me you broke some ribs."

"Naw," he said, waving a hand in dismissal. "Turns out they're just bruised. They gave me some really good drugs, though." His gaze dropped to her knees. "Stitches, huh?"

"Yeah. And no showers for yet another week."

He smiled at her. She managed to smile back. Another man hovered in the background, and at the uncomfortable silence he stood and walked toward her. He held out his hand.

"Danny Anderson," he said by way of introduction. "From what Dylan tells me, I missed a damn good voyage. Can't say I'm sorry I did, though, looking at the two of you."

Casey managed a weak laugh. She remembered Daniel as the man who had promised to drive her van up here. "So, how's Bessie?"

"Bessie?"

"Her van," Dylan explained.

"Oh. Well..." He rubbed the back of his neck. "I can't say it's good as new."

"I didn't ask for a miracle," she said. "I just want it running."

"Well, it's running."

"That's all I ever ask of Bessie."

An awkward silence ensued. She couldn't seem to look at Dylan, though she felt his gaze hot on her. Danny just stared at both of them, one after the other.

"Well," Danny said finally, clapping his hands together, "I'm sure the two of you would love to stay in this hospital for the rest of the night, but I'm supposed to bring you to the surprise party they're holding at the hotel." He headed toward the exit. "The MacCabes have been waiting for you for three days. If we don't go now, there will be none of Pappy's punch left for either of you."

They arrived less than a half hour later. True to form, the MacCabes had taken over the small hotel lobby for the party. A glittering Welcome Home banner hung across the entrance. They'd twisted brown-and-orange bunting all over the lobby and pinned up pictures of pilgrims and turkeys on every spare inch of wall. Dylan's brother had dressed up in buckskins and every woman who could had plaited her hair in two braids. It looked like a kids' Thanksgiving Day party.

It would be quite a while, Casey realized, before she would get to lie down alone in silence.

The cameras started flashing as soon as they limped through the door. Someone thrust a cup of punch in her hand—a punch, Casey noticed, that had been liberally spiked. The noise quickly reached rock-concert levels and she did her best to nod and smile at all the vaguely familiar faces. Dylan and she soon got separated in the crush.

Somebody thrust a key into her hand. Apparently, Dylan's family had rented every room in the hotel and saved a room each for her and for Dylan. Casey thanked the woman—she thought it might be Anne, Dylan's sister—and put the key in her pocket. She curled her fingers around the key and fantasized about a long, hot bath and a wide, soft bed.

Then the crowd parted and she caught sight of Dylan wheeling an elderly man toward her. She glanced down at the man's wizened face, at the thick woolen blanket covering his knees, and realized who this man must be.

"Casey, I'd like you to meet my grandfather." Dylan came around and perched on the edge of the lobby couch. "Grandpa," he said, raising his voice above the noise, "this is Casey. She came with me on the trip. Down the old trail from Canada."

"I've heard so much about you, Mr. MacCabe." Casey leaned forward and held out her hand. He tilted his head and peered at her through his glasses, which magnified his eyes enough so Casey could see where Dylan got his deep blue eyes. Dylan's grandfather rifled his hand out from under the blanket, took her hand, and held it. Then, with surprising strength, he pulled it to his mouth for a kiss.

Around her came tsking and cries of "Grandpa!" The elderly man grinned, a grin that Casey was sure, in his younger years, had made many a fair maiden fall.

"Did Dylan tell you that we found your marker, Mr. MacCabe? It's still standing."

"'Course, 'course." He nodded, his voice croaky and low. "No other way t'find Morgan's Pass."

She lifted a brow at Dylan. She'd thought his grandfather had long ago lost his memory, but it was clear he knew what she was talking about.

"I'm going to write about it, you know," she said. "For a magazine. It'll be a wonderful story."

Dylan's grandfather continued to look at her and smile, then he beckoned to Dylan to come closer. Dylan leaned in.

"A pretty one," his grandfather said, raising a hand toward Casey. "Which wife is this?"

Casey stiffened. Around them, the family tittered, but it was a nervous sort of laughter. Dylan didn't smile. He looked at Casey and held her gaze, then leaned even closer to his grandfather.

"The last one, Grandpa," Dylan whispered, loud enough for only the three of them to hear. "The last one, I hope."

12

"JILLIAN," CASEY SAID into the phone. "You are *not* help-ing."

"Help? Of course, I'm helping." Casey heard the distinct sound of Jillian sucking on a cigarette. "It's ten o'clock, I'm alone in my Manhattan apartment, and I'm spending my Friday night listening to you. Believe me, that's helping."

Casey closed her eyes and pinched the bridge of her nose. She swung her bare legs off the bed and curled her toes in the knotty hotel-room carpet. She'd been on the phone for so long that her hair was dry after the bath, and so far Jillian didn't have a word of wisdom for her. "I need advice, Jillian. I need guidance. Isn't that what I'm paying you for?"

"No, kid, you're paying me to listen. And what I'm hear-ing sounds like one of my other patient's fantasies."

"Jillian!"

"Listen to yourself!" she exclaimed, and Casey could vi-sualize her stubbing out yet another half-smoked cigarette. "You just spent three weeks playing voyageur in the gran-deur of the northern woods with some hunky mountain man and *you* want *my* help?"

"It's not that simple—"

"Honey, why don't we turn the tables for a minute and have you give me some advice. Where did you find this guy?"

"I told you, I had to interview him on assignment."

"I'm in the wrong business," she complained. "All I see is whining neurotics and men who want to cheat on their wives. Do you know how hard it is for a woman over thirty to find a single man—hell, any man—in New York City?"

"But you don't understand. This guy is *serious*." Casey jerked up off the bed and started to pace in a tight little circle, tethered to the hotel nightstand by the short phone cord. "He's thinking long-term." She curled her arm around her middle, remembering his words at the party, remembering the way he'd looked at her. "At least, I think he is."

"Is that a bad thing?"

"Well..."

"Casey, are you sure you didn't get knocked on the head when that boat capsized? 'Cause you're sounding pretty demented right now."

"Why? A guy wants to get involved with me—after all these years—and I'm supposed to be okay with this?"

"Hear this, Casey?"

Casey stilled and listened to the silence. "What? I don't hear anything."

"It's the world's smallest violin."

Casey planted a fist on her hip. "You know, you could turn down that city sarcasm for a minute or so. It might make you seem more sympathetic."

"From where I'm sitting in my big empty water bed, it's real hard to muscle up sympathy for your plight, you know what I mean?"

Casey sighed. "I shouldn't have called—"

"Wait! Wait!" Jillian growled in frustration and then gave a familiar long-suffering sigh. "Don't hang up, kid. I shouldn't be loading you with my problems. Just—don't hang up."

Casey sank down on the bed. She thrust her fingers

through her hair. It felt funny against her hand, soft and clean, and when she let it go it fell into her eyes. She needed a cut. These past weeks, she'd gotten used to having bits of leaves fall from it. She'd gotten used to wearing it up, away from her face.

She'd gotten used to a lot of wonderful things, if she let herself think about them. She'd gotten used to having Dylan around. She glanced at the Spartan furnishings of the hotel room: the burnt orange carpeting, the stucco walls, the generic sailboat print. This was the first hour in almost a month that she'd been without him. She felt strange. Dislocated.

Maybe she shouldn't have called. Jillian was right. She was being whiny. Ungrateful. She was complaining about a situation other women dreamed of. But not every woman had lived her life. Not every woman knew how hard it was to rebuild castles in the air.

She heard Jillian rustling. Then she heard the sound of a lighter scraping up a flame, the suck of smoke into her therapist's lungs.

Casey murmured, "You really should give up that dirty habit."

"I am. I'm down to two packs a day."

"Great. Now you'll be fifty when you die instead of forty-five."

"Hey, I'll leave a prettier corpse."

Casey managed a smile. It was a familiar back-and-forth between them. A little comfortable repartee, Jillian would call it, to ease the social awkwardness.

Then, on an exhale, Jillian said, "Okay, Casey. It seems to me that your 'problem' boils down to one simple question."

Casey sank back down on the bed. "Well, what is it?"

"Do you love him?"

The question caught her unprepared. She sat there as the words rippled through her consciousness. Truth be told, she'd asked herself that question a hundred times and she already knew the answer, but she was having a hard time saying it aloud. She was having a hard time *thinking* it.

Jillian's voice came through loud and clear. "Hmm. That's just what I thought."

"But I didn't say anything yet."

"I know. If you'd answered right away, one way or another, then I'd know you had problems."

"Well," Casey remarked, "that makes no sense."

"It makes all the sense in the world. You're not jumping into a relationship. You're thinking about it—and thinking about it hard. That means I'm archiving your file."

"What?"

"Casey, there comes a time a therapist dreams of: sending a patient out on her own. I'm pushing you out of the nest."

"Jillian!"

"Honey, you don't need me anymore. Not as a counselor, anyway. There's not a person in the whole wide world who can help you when it comes to love. This woodsman is either 'the one' or he isn't, and the only one who knows the answer to that question is you."

Casey closed her eyes and lay back on the bed, letting her head sink into the pillows. Jillian. She loved Jillian. For all her wisecracking and irreverence, the lady always knew how to cut through the smoke right to the fire.

"Heck, Jillian," Casey murmured. "You're good."

"I know." Casey heard the scrape of an ashtray as Jillian stubbed out another cigarette. "I expect to be invited to the wedding, by the way. And if you decide you don't want him, give him my number. Tell him I'll play Pocahontas to his Capt. John Smith anytime."

CASEY HAD JUST HUNG UP the phone after talking with her sister when Dylan knocked on the door.

She knew it was Dylan, though she couldn't see through the closed drapes. She'd been expecting him all night. She'd been bracing herself for this all night.

She opened the door and peered around the edge. Dylan stood with his hands deep in his pockets. He'd changed into crisp, clean khakis and a polo shirt. He looked freshly showered. Clean-shaven. Distinctly uncertain.

"Hi," he said.

"Hi." She backed up and inched the door open, then spread her arm out in invitation. "Come on in."

He walked in and spent a little time looking around the room, though she knew her room must be just like his—she knew from long experience that all hotel rooms looked alike—and there wasn't anything particularly fascinating about the spread of her things on the chairs and bureau. She felt like asking him if he wanted anything to drink, until she realized all she had to offer was a diet soda she'd opened hours ago, which had undoubtedly gone flat.

He paused and glanced at her over his shoulder as the door clicked shut.

"Nice party," she murmured, leaning back against the door, intensely self-conscious about the ratty white bathrobe she wore. "You've got...quite a family."

"Yeah."

"It sounds like it's still going strong."

"Uh-huh. They'll probably have to call in the Mounties to break it up." His gaze drifted over her, then settled on her bandaged knees. "How are the stitches?"

"Itchy," she said. "Tight. How are the ribs?"

"Dull. The painkillers are doing their job."

"Good. Glad you didn't break anything."

"Me, too."

She looked away from him, and found the pattern of worn spots on the old carpet of intense interest. Strange, how they could be so awkward with each other. Only this afternoon, they'd made love on a riverbank with nothing beneath them but the soft grass and nothing above but sunshine. Now they stood together, alone in a hotel bedroom, and it was as if the St. Lawrence River stretched between them.

"So," he said, thrusting his hands more deeply into his pockets and rocking back on his heels, "I think this is when you tell me that it's been a nice couple of weeks, thank you very much, but you're heading out tomorrow for another assignment."

Casey stilled. She met his gaze. She'd spent a lot of time wondering what was going to happen here tonight. She'd spent a lot of time worrying that he would fall to his knees and confess undying love, beg her to be wife number three. She'd spent most of her time composing what she would say if he did.

Now, she felt vaguely disappointed that he *hadn't*.

"C'mon, Casey," he said, irritation clear in his voice. "Stop giving me that deer-caught-in-the-headlights look. It's been nearly twelve hours since the canoe capsized. And you didn't have any of Pappy's punch at the party. You've had long enough to clear your head."

"My head's clear enough."

First lie of the night. Her mind *wasn't* clear. She'd spent most of the evening trying to blow out the smoke. She wasn't quite sure what she was going to do—but she was sure of one thing: She wanted no bitterness between them. She cared for Dylan far too much for that.

"I almost didn't come here tonight. I don't need to hear this, you know." He walked toward the bureau and leaned back against it. "I've been around long enough to see the signs. You've been dodging me all night, hell, all *day*. So let's get this over with, swift and clean, so we both can get on with our lives.''

Her voice came out as a whisper. ''Is that what you want, Dylan?''

''Hell, no.'' He looked away from her and pushed off from the bureau. He paced a tight little circle in the space between the bed and the chest of drawers. ''But I'll be damned if I'm going to stand here and rip out my heart just so you can stuff it back in me again.''

A quiver ran through her. It softened her knees. She sank against the door at her back and felt the ribs of the molding press into her shoulder blades.

''There's nothing I can say, Casey, that's going to change this.'' He balled his hands into fists in his pockets. ''Either you feel it, or you don't. Either you want it, or you're going to run away from it. At this stage of the game, there's not a damn thing I can say to convince you, one way or the other.''

He was hurting, too, Casey realized. He couldn't even meet her eyes. She remembered, suddenly, when she'd first found out he'd had two other wives. How she'd thought ill of him—a man who fell breezily in and out of love, a man who made light of commitments. Looking at this angry man pacing in her room she began to understand the full extent of the pain he'd suffered.

She also realized that he would want all or nothing from her, and she wasn't sure she was ready for either.

''Damn it, Casey, say something.'' He took two paces toward her, angry fierce steps. ''Tell me you want me to stay. Or tell me you want me to go. Just tell me *something*.''

''Stay.''

The word lurched out of her, a dangerous whisper, but loud enough for him to hear. His eyes brightened, his body stiffened, and in a moment he was in front of her, framing her face with his hands.

"Stay, Dylan," she repeated, as her body grew soft and languid. "Stay...for tonight."

His fingers froze in her hair. The light in his eyes grew cold. He leaned back from her and it was as if he'd retreated a hundred thousand miles.

She seized his wrists to keep him still, to keep him close. His arms felt as hard as iron beneath her grip. "Listen to me, Dylan. Please. This isn't easy for me, either." He stayed near her, but his look grew wary, guarded. She flexed her fingers over his wrists. "I've known you for three weeks, Dylan. Three weeks. And it's been wild and fierce and intense—it's been a whirlwind. I hardly know where my head is right now, I hardly know what to think."

"Stop thinking and *feel*."

"I know what I feel." Her voice dropped to a whisper, though there was no one else in the room. "I know that I want you. I want you now, and I want you here, in this bed."

He made a strange sound in the back of his throat. He framed her face with his hands again. She felt the press of his hips, so close to her own loins.

"I'm not looking for lust, lady. That's too easy."

"I know." She loosened her grip on his wrists. She let her hands fall to the tie of her bathrobe, and loosened it until the terry cloth fell open and the air brushed her skin. "All I'm asking is that it be enough...for now."

He pressed his forehead against hers, and looked down past her face, toward her breasts. She felt his hot gaze upon her skin. He made a strange, tortured sound, braced his forearms on either side of her head and grazed his lips against her temple. "Damn, Casey, why are you doing this to me?"

"I want you, Dylan." She wrapped her arms around his neck and spoke into his hair. "I need you."

"You're leaving in the morning."

"Yes," she admitted, in a small, breathy voice. "Yes..."

He pulled away from her and stared at her with angry eyes. "So you are leaving."

"I promised my sister I'd visit," she said softly. "And I need some time alone. To think."

"So what's this?" he demanded angrily. "The goodbye f—"

"Don't." She silenced the ugly word with her fingers. "Don't say that, Dylan. Don't you know me better than that? I'm leaving tomorrow morning, but it doesn't have to be forever."

He stared at her for a long time, and Casey looked steadily into those angry blue eyes, feeling her will crumble as each moment passed, wondering if she shouldn't just collapse into a quivering heap at his feet and beg him to let her stay.... But no, no, she couldn't. She'd known Charlie five years before they'd married. She'd known this man three weeks. She needed to make sure that this was the real thing, and not just a hot infatuation born of isolation and danger. She needed time and space and a lot of deep, cleansing breaths—away from Dylan's magnetic presence, away from his hot bed.

Then he pressed his face against hers again and slipped his hands beneath the terry cloth to curl in the hollow of her back. "This isn't going to be easy, you know."

"I know," she whispered, as he pulled her into his embrace.

"The sex, I mean," he said. "The doctor warned me against all strenuous activity."

She pulled away long enough to smile gently into his eyes. She saw a lot in those eyes. A lot of pain. A lot of words left unsaid. And a lot of yearning that matched her own.

"Well," she replied, "I'll just have to get on top of the situation."

"On top, eh?" He glanced down the length of her body. "What about those knees?"

"Oh...yeah." She pouted as she visualized the problems. "I forgot about the knees."

"It looks like we're going to have to be very, very careful."

"Hmm," she murmured as he brushed his lips against the sensitive spot just below her ear. "And very, very inventive."

Then, just before he touched his lips to hers, he held her head still. He waited for her to blink her eyes back open.

"Take some time, Casey," he said. "But just remember: I won't wait forever."

"IT'S ALL RIGHT, BESSIE." Casey smoothed her hand over the dashboard of her minivan as the vehicle hiccuped its way through Bridgewater. "That looks like the center of town ahead—it won't be long now."

Casey pressed the brake as she approached a traffic light. A cluster of amber leaves danced across the windshield, buoyed by a cool September breeze. She glanced at the crinkled map tossed haphazardly on the passenger seat, then quickly glanced away, to the bundle of official-looking brick buildings just ahead. The map had led her to the town of Bridgewater, but for what she was looking for, she was on her own now. She was working on pure instinct.

She flexed her fingers over the steering wheel, waiting for the light to turn green. She glanced at the dashboard clock. She'd been driving for seven hours. She'd developed a cramp in her calf from pressing the gas pedal, and a crick in her neck from keeping her eyes on the road. But she wasn't about to stop now. She was too close. It had taken her three years to run away, and now, it had taken her exactly three weeks to find her way home. She didn't want to wait another moment.

A few blocks ahead, she spied the library. In these old towns, the library was never lover far from the school, so she drove the roads around it in a two-block radius. Sure enough, she soon came upon a large red-brick building with the name Bridgewater High School carved above the granite-columned entrance.

She pulled the van into a space in front and stretched out of the vehicle. Rolling her shoulders, she walked toward the imposing building, quelling an unexpected tickle of uncertainty. He'd said he wouldn't wait forever...but three weeks was hardly forever.

To Casey, they'd been the longest three weeks of her life. Not for lack of something to do, though. She'd thought she would never finish her article for *American Backroads*. She'd thought the days she'd spent with her sister and her kids would never end, and the few days she'd spent with her parents in her own hometown had stretched even longer. Added to that another assignment in Virginia.... She'd been busy, but it didn't matter. Every night she'd thought of Dylan. Every night she'd considered picking up the phone, then thought of an excuse not to. Every night she'd considered coming back here to do exactly what she was doing now.

She announced herself at the office and got a visitor's badge, then followed the secretary's directions through the stark, echoing halls to "Mr. MacCabe's" classroom. Then, looking through the wired glass toward the man lecturing by the blackboard in front of a classroom full of rapt students, she stilled. The tickle of uncertainty strengthened.

He'd cut his hair. Gone were the wild, unruly locks of the summertime. He'd trimmed it short and neat, a style that brought out the angle of his cheekbones and the squareness of his clean-shaven jaw. He'd wrapped his broad shoulders in a crisp oxford-cloth shirt. A muted tie was knotted neatly at his throat. The cotton of his shirt billowed above the leather belt looped through his crisp khaki pants. She couldn't be sure, but she suspected that tassels swung on his leather loafers.

She sucked a slow and uncertain breath into her lungs, for this was the man she knew and loved—transformed into someone she didn't quite recognize.

But of course, that was an illusion. Did she expect him to be teaching in tank tops and biker's shorts? Dylan was Dylan, no matter how he dressed. He was still the man who had made wild love to her on river banks under the summer sun all over northern New York State. He was still the man who had taught her not to be afraid of loving. He was still the man who had led her, gently, step-by-step, through her fears.

She waited until the bell rang, then she slipped through the door. She sensed the curious gazes of more than a few students as they rushed past her, but she ignored them and wound her way through the desks toward where Dylan stood, erasing the blackboard.

"Dylan?"

His shoulders tensed. The eraser paused in midair. He swiveled on one foot, and then all she could see were Dylan's Viking eyes and the river of emotions that ran through them.

Her throat closed up; she couldn't speak. She could hardly breathe. In a flash of a moment it was as if she were transported from this stuffy classroom to some wooded hillside, with the gurgle of a river nearby. In the space of a breath, she was alive again.

She didn't know how long they stood like that, staring at each other, speaking in silent tongues. Eventually, she became aware of the noise coming from the hall; the sound of students laughing and slamming lockers and calling out after-school plans to one another. Dylan walked to the door and closed it, shutting it all out.

When he turned around to face her, the spell was broken. His eyes went blank. As if a shade had been pulled down across them.

"Where's your hallway pass, young lady?" Dylan stood, one hand braced against the door, the other on his hip. "You're late for class."

"Not too late, I hope."

"Late enough to earn a detention."

"Well..." She sauntered through the row of desks toward him. "I want to be detained, anyway. At least for a little while."

He crossed his arms and stood there, his legs spread, his eyes hooded and wary. "I just saw the October edition of *American Backroads,*" he said. "Our story isn't in it. Are you coming to tell me they've changed their minds and decided not to run it?"

"No." Casey shrugged. "I didn't make the October deadline, with our delay and all. It'll be in the November issue."

"I see."

He wove his fingers through his hair and Casey's heart stopped. She remembered that reflexive, nervous gesture. She'd seen him do that before—a hundred times before—and for a moment she imagined she smelled the scent of pine and heard leaves rustling around them.

Then he glanced up at her with a look in his eyes that she remembered.

"I'd just about given up on you, Casey Michaels," he said.

"Oh, Dylan," she said softly, pausing at the last row of desks. "You didn't think I was going to leave every-thing...just like that."

"Yeah, I did."

"No, I couldn't. I...couldn't." She trailed a finger along the battered wood of a desk. "I needed time. I told you I'd stay away. I'd told myself I'd stay away for at least as long as I'd been with you, to see if the fires cooled."

"Well?"

He said the word on a growl, and looked at her with a gaze that could make water take flame. The long-sleeved linen suit and the simple cotton vest she'd worn under it now seemed much too warm for the cool late-September weather.

Her heart rose to her throat, for this was the moment she'd dreamed of these past weeks. She'd told herself she would just open her mouth and let him know exactly how she felt, exactly what he'd come to mean to her. But in her dreams this part was fuzzy and swift, and segued quickly into the moment when he took her in his arms and made hungry love to her against the blackboard.

The words stuck in her throat. There were no words, re-ally. There was just a feeling, just a realization—that in life bad things would always happen, and those were out of her control. But she would only experience the good things in life if she actively went out and conquered her fear and seized them. She'd been with Dylan long enough to know that staring into her own fear was a small price to pay for a whole lot of happiness.

She knew she couldn't just let the words remain unspo-ken. He needed to hear them. He'd suffered, too. His knuckles were white against the door, his jaw tight. He was holding back, waiting for her.

"I've been thinking," she said, her voice strangely breathless, "about settling down somewhere for a while."

He made a sound, a strange sucking sound. A muscle flexed in his cheek.

"I'm getting tired of traveling all over the country," she admitted. "And Bessie's just about ready to be put to pasture. I'm...I'm thinking of doing newspaper work again. Maybe local work."

Still, he didn't move. He didn't budge.

"The editor of my hometown paper told me I can have my job back whenever I want."

"In Morristown."

"Yes," she said. "I'm thinking about starting a book, too. About my travels—"

"You mentioned that when we were together. Something about stories of the people you've met."

"Yes. You remember."

"There ain't a hell of a lot of those three weeks I can forget."

"Me, either."

A charged moment passed. Casey met his gaze and the journey swept before their eyes—the day he'd washed her hair in the cove, the lovemaking on the riverbank, the soft evenings in the tent—and she knew that nothing had cooled between them, that time had only made her ache for him more.

Why had she ever expected otherwise?

He dropped his hand from the door and shifted his stance. "I suppose Morristown isn't so far. What, five, six hours from here?"

"I turned down the job offer, Dylan." She shrugged. An image of the little white house she and Charlie had lived in flashed through her mind...then faded, slowly, sweetly, like the end of a dream. "I've decided to find a job elsewhere, to start a whole new life."

A light sparked in his eye, but still he held himself tight. "Bridgewater has a fine weekly," he said. "I know they'd appreciate having a writer of your experience on staff."

"I love you, Dylan."

She'd spoken softly. But loud enough for him to hear. His eyes widened and he stared at her as if she'd just levitated.

"I love you," she repeated, the surety strong in her heart. "I loved you three weeks ago, too, but I didn't have the courage then to say it. I love you, and I hope it isn't too late—"

He crossed the distance between them in the blink of an eye. Cupping her head in his hands, he kissed her words away. Kissed her hard. Slanted his face against hers until she could feel the first prickle of the shadow of his beard. And all the world dissolved around her in a rush of color and light.

Much later, breathless and trembling, she blinked open her eyes to see Dylan's smile as wide as the St. Lawrence River.

"You're trying to get me in trouble, right?" he said, hoarsely. "Get me thrown out for committing a lewd act on school property, right? Then I'll have to live with you in that beat-up van of yours and travel around like a gypsy—"

"Hey," she said, between breaths, "you're the one who started kissing me—"

"Because there's no way a woman who has lived a life like yours wants to be stuck in a backwater town with a guy like me, raising a passel of kids and spending summers in a log cabin—"

"Going to football games in the fall and growing tomatoes," she added, tears filling her eyes. "Ice fishing in the winter and barbecuing in the summer."

His hands curved around her head and he shook her gently. "What the hell took you so long to figure everything out?

"I had to slow down, Dylan. I've been running for so long." She spread her hands across his chest. "The only running I want to do, from now on, is running an editor's desk at the *Bridgewater Weekly*. And maybe a bake sale for the Girl Scouts."

"Are you sure?"

"Yes," she said, and she felt the glow of certainty light up her face. "I've never been more sure about anything in my life."

"Then marry me, Casey Michaels."

"Yes."

Yes. A song lilted in her heart. Tears fell shamelessly down her cheeks. *Yes, yes, yes.* Heedless of the dirty floor, heedless of the noise of students outside the door, she fell to her knees with him, then pressed her face against his shoulder. Dylan wrapped his arms around her. Strong arms. Sure arms.

A little while later, they made their way, hand in hand, out of the school to a more private place. Casey looked up at him with the sun on his hair and the light of love in his eyes. Yes, she thought. Life had a way of shifting under her feet when she least expected it...but this time, she had landed on air.

FANTASY Lori Foster

Blaze

Brandi Sommers had just been given the most outrageous
birthday present. Her sister, Shay, had been to a charity
auction—and bought her a man! Gorgeous bodyguard Sebastian
Sinclair was Brandi's slave for five whole days—what *was* she
going to do with him?

MANHUNTING IN MANHATTAN Carolyn Andrews

Manhunting

As Carly Carpenter flew home to her sister's wedding, she
decided it was time to find herself a man. But it seemed her
sister, Jenna, already had things in hand: she'd dropped the
perfect man right in Carly's lap—her own fiancé!

LOVING WILD Lisa Ann Verge

Dylan MacCabe was a man with a mission and he needed Casey
Michaels to help him complete it. His first problem was
convincing Casey of that. His second was working out how he
was going to spend three weeks with her, sleeping under the
stars, and not follow Nature's course...

THE GETAWAY GROOM Molly Liholm

Megan Cooper's nuptials were just another assignment for
wedding consultant Emma Delaney. Until Emma met Megan's
fiancé! The sexy groom was the same man who had left Emma at
the altar eight years ago. Could she really plan his marriage to
another woman?

CHRISTMAS

Affairs

MORE THAN JUST KISSES UNDER THE MISTLETOE...

Enjoy three sparkling seasonal romances by your
favourite authors from

MILLS & BOON®
Presents™

HELEN BIANCHIN
For Anique, the season of goodwill has become...
The Seduction Season

SANDRA MARTON
Can Santa weave a spot of Christmas magic for Nick
and Holly in... *A Miracle on Christmas Eve?*

SHARON KENDRICK
Will Aleck and Clemmie have a... *Yuletide Reunion?*

MILLS & BOON®

Makes any time special™

Available from 6th November 1998

MARGOT DALTON

second thoughts

To Detective Jackie Kaminsky it seemed like a routine
burglary, until she took a second look at the
evidence... The intruder knew his way around
Maribel Lewis's home—yet took nothing.
He *seems* to know Maribel's deepest secret—
and wants payment in blood.

A spellbinding new Kaminsky mystery.

1-55166-421-6
**AVAILABLE IN PAPERBACK
FROM OCTOBER, 1998**

Jennifer
BLAKE

KANE

Down in Louisiana, family comes first.
That's the rule the Benedicts live by.
So when a beautiful redhead starts paying a little
too much attention to Kane Benedict's grandfather,
Kane decides to find out what her *real* motives are.

"Blake's style is as steamy as a still July night...as overwhelming hot as Cajun spice."

—Chicago Times

1-55166-429-1
**AVAILABLE IN PAPERBACK
FROM OCTOBER, 1998**

FIND THE FRUIT!

How would you like to win a year's supply of Mills & Boon®
Books—FREE! Well, if you know your fruit, then you're
already one step ahead when it comes to completing this
competition, because all the answers are fruit! Simply
decipher the code to find the names of ten fruit,
complete the coupon overleaf and send it to us by 30th April 1999.
The first five correct entries will each win a year's subscription to the
Mills & Boon series of their choice. What could be easier?

A	B	C	D	E	F	G	H	I
15					20			

J	K	L	M	N	O	P	Q	R
	25						5	

S	T	U	V	W	X	Y	Z
			10				

4	19	15	17	22

15	10	3	17	15	18	3

2	19	17	8	15	6	23	2	19

4	19	15	6

4	26	9	1

7	8	6	15	11	16	19	6	6	13

3	6	15	2	21	19

15	4	4	26	19

1	15	2	21	3

16	15	2	15	2	15

C8J

Please turn over for details of how to enter ➜

HOW TO ENTER

There are ten coded words listed overleaf, which when decoded each spell the name of a fruit. There is also a grid which contains each letter of the alphabet and a number has been provided under some of the letters. All you have to do, is complete the grid, by working out which number corresponds with each letter of the alphabet. When you have done this, you will be able to decipher the coded words to discover the names of the ten fruit! As you decipher each code, write the name of the fruit in the space provided, then fill in the coupon below, pop this page into an envelope and post it today. Don't forget you could win a year's supply of Mills & Boon® Books—you don't even need to pay for a stamp!

Mills & Boon Find the Fruit Competition
FREEPOST CN81, Croydon, Surrey, CR9 3WZ
EIRE readers: (please affix stamp) PO Box 4546, Dublin 24.

Please tick the series you would like to receive if you are one of the lucky winners

Presents™ ❏ Enchanted™ ❏ Medical Romance™ ❏
Historical Romance™ ❏ Temptation® ❏

Are you a Reader Service™ subscriber?   Yes ❏   No ❏

Ms/Mrs/Miss/Mr ....Initials ....
                                        (BLOCK CAPITALS PLEASE)

Surname...

Address ....

....

....Postcode..........................

(I am over 18 years of age)   C8J